SHOW UP

SERAPH'S BURLESQUE CLUB

RENÉE DAHLIA

Show Up
Renee Dahlia

A fake date … a real secret

An invitation to her ex's wedding is the icing on a crappy cake for burlesque dancer Yolande. Her ex ghosted her just as they were about to take the stage for their neo-burlesque act. Yolande's friends at Seraph's Burlesque Club persuade her that attending will show her ex that she's moved on. She just needs a date.

Shy bartender Reiko has a secret, or two. She can't risk anyone discovering that her life as a penniless PhD student and bartender is a sham. And even though she's been in love with Yolande since forever, when Yolande needs a plus-one to save face at her ex's wedding, Reiko knows any fantasy of romance is just that - fantasy. Yolande will never notice the way Reiko looks at her.

When the drama of the wedding reveals a spark of attraction between them, Reiko will have to risk her fake identity for the hope of real love.

- found family
    - fake dating
    - friends to lovers
    - only one bed

ABOUT THE AUTHOR

Renée Dahlia is an unabashed romance reader who loves feisty women and strong, clever men. Her books reflect this, with a side note of awkward humour. Renée has a science degree in physics. When not distracted by the characters fighting for attention in her brain, she works in the horse-racing industry doing data analysis and writing magazine articles. When she isn't reading or writing, Renée spends her time with her partner and four children, usually watching them play cricket.

For everyone with multiple careers who don't really know what they want to do with their life. It's okay not to know.

FOREWORD

Welcome to SHOW UP, the first book in the Seraph's Burlesque Club series.

This series consists of three lesbian romances is set in a burlesque club in London. If you love to read about a found family with queer people who thrive, this series has that and more. This book is friends to lovers with a high heat level, fake dating, only one bed, and a fun heist.

Please note that this book is set in a post-COVID London where everyone is vaccinated. There will be some references to the pandemic. There are also references to a character's mother dying in a car crash prior to the book, and a minor discussion of racism.

If you are keen to keep up to date on new releases and, more importantly, sales, I recommend you sign up to my newsletter, or follow me on social media or at romance.com.au

I hope you enjoy reading this book!
Renée

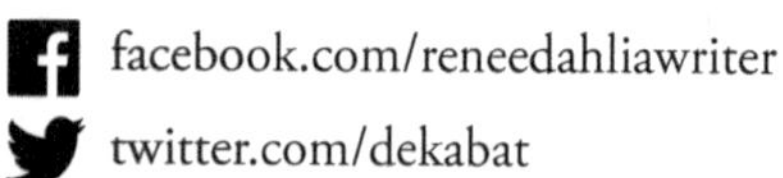

facebook.com/reneedahliawriter

twitter.com/dekabat

instagram.com/reneedahlia_author

bookbub.com/authors/renee-dahlia

1

"Can you grab some more beers from the store room before Yolande and Helen go on?"

Reiko nodded in response to Steph's question and walked away from the noise of a busy Seraph's Burlesque Club, down the hallway towards the cold store room out the back of the bar. Londoners had embraced being allowed to go back to the pub with a vengeance. If people had ever doubted Londoners' love for a drink with friends, there was no doubt now. The club scene thrived, and most people weren't fussed about having to show their digital vaccination card before entering, because at least they could get out of their bloody homes.

Yolande and Helen were one of the most popular acts, with many regulars who would need refreshments after their set. Their modern neo-burlesque style with Helen in top hat and tails while Yolande wore frilly summer frocks quickly became an act of bondage as they revealed the leather corsets and steam-punk chains underneath. Crowds loved them. Each layer of their dance had wide appeal, especially with the groups of young men who fetishized lesbians. Ahh well, burlesque was all about the tease and those young men spent a good amount of money every evening. Reiko, like all the staff here, was adept at ignoring that nonsense. And while they were the worst part of the crowd, there were many others who genuinely loved watching two women kiss; people like Reiko who could only be free to be herself here at Seraph's. Was it really freedom if she kept secrets wherever she went? Her family didn't know about this part of her life and her friends had no clue who her family was, and her PhD supervisor knew nothing about her at all.

Reiko picked up the box of expensive craft beer bottles from the cold store and made her way along the narrow corridor past the dancer's dressing rooms back to the bar. A wail rang out from one of the dressing rooms, and she paused to listen. If she had to bet, she'd guess the hysterical sobs came from Yolande, although that made zero sense because she'd bounced in here happy to be back on stage with Helen.

Yolande being upset was so out of character that Reiko almost dropped the case of beer she carried. Reiko loved Yolande's enthusiasm for life. During the hardest parts of the lockdown, Yolande's joie de vivre had kept them all from the pits of despair over the plight of the world. She placed the beer on the floor and leaned against the wall, ready to help.

"You can't let her bad choice ruin your act." The calm voice from Seraph's owner, Beth, belied her words. Whose bad choice? Helen's?

"But she's gone. Forever. I loved her." Yolande sobbed, each word cutting at Reiko's heart. Helen had quit dancing? Reiko gasped—not just quit dancing—by the sound of

Yolande's anguish, Helen must be injured or even dead. Gone. That's what Yolande said. Reiko wanted to rush in there and wrap Yolande up in a big hug, but she scoffed at herself. Yolande's relationship wasn't her business. Reiko was just the kitty, who picked up all the discarded costumes and did all the awful jobs no one else wanted. She was everyone's shoulder to cry on, their friend when needed, and the quiet one who everyone ignored when they didn't need her. Damn, she sounded bitter. A little unrequited admiration for Yolande shouldn't unbalance her like that. She chose this job and she loved it here. She leaned down to pick up the beers and get back to work.

"Get on stage and prove her wrong. She left and you can do this without her." Beth's sharp tone cut through Yolande's sob. It stopped Reiko mid-bend. How catastrophic of her to assume Helen was dead. She'd quit. Like Beth said, Helen had made a bad choice. What dreadful timing. Reiko wanted to say that she'd never liked Helen anyway, but it wasn't true. Helen could be a pain in the arse at times, but she was usually nice to everyone. The reality was that Reiko had always been jealous of Helen. Helen, who got to kiss Yolande and go home with her after the show. Helen, who had amazing tits and a glamorous body. Serenity Busts was Helen's stage name, and her Christmas special where she'd pole-danced to a remix featuring the famous Seinfeld Serenity Now joke had been one of their most popular online shows.

"Come on. Wash your face. Let's do your makeup and then you can go out there and slay the crowd. Give them the show of your life, and afterwards, Reiko or Steph will make you a drink. You can cry later." Beth's no-nonsense approach must have worked because there were no more sobs. A guilty flush tracked over the back of Reiko's neck. She shouldn't have heard any of that; it was none of her business. She picked up the case of beer and hustled back to the bar.

"What took you so long?" Steph looked a bit stressed.

"Sorry." Reiko opened the box and stacked the beers in the fridge behind the bar. When she stood up, she blinked. Crowds lined the bar. "Hi, who is next?" She smiled at the group of people lining the bar and got to work.

Hours later, Reiko's feet ached, and she wanted to sit down and take off her practical shoes. She should book a massage, or a pedicure, or both for tomorrow to soothe her sore feet. Standing all evening wasn't the best for her feet or her back. She heard the whisper of Mum's voice asking why she did it when she didn't have to, and she welcomed the slight ache in preference to her family's expectations for her life.

"Well done, Reiko." Steph held up her palm and Reiko gave her a half-hearted high five.

"It's good to be busy." It really was, and her sore feet were a good reminder that Seraph's Burlesque Club might just survive. She needed this place as much as it needed her; this was her found family. Everyone made her feel welcome in a way that her family didn't, and she'd never really felt like she belonged in her other work either. She shook off the usual annoyance at her PhD supervisor. Things were supposed to be better now that she was a doctoral student; she had more autonomy over her research. Yes, she'd picked a topic that wasn't very fashionable or popular, but it mattered to her. It was trendy to be vegan, and yet many of the most popular influencers were hugely problematic. A couple of years ago, when the Black Lives Matter movement had peaked, it'd been easy to convince her supervisor that it would be worthwhile to investigate racism among the vegan movement, but now everyone wanted to pretend that racism had been solved and her research was suddenly deemed irrelevant. All of which meant it was more relevant than ever before. She sighed; being here at Seraph's gave her a break from the stress of having to prove her topic worthy.

"Hey, we just pulled a record take tonight." Beth bundled Steph into a hug. "You did a great job managing the bar. That's our best taking since… before." Everyone knew what the pause meant; before the pandemic had fucked everything. The whole world had some form of PTSD, Reiko was sure of it, and the ongoing nuances and impacts would keep social science and psychotherapy researchers busy for years.

"It was a team effort. Poor Reiko must have done a million trips to the store room tonight to keep the front bar stocked. And Jack's show really held the crowd together after Yolande's disaster."

"Steph." Reiko didn't want to hear anyone talk negatively about Yolande after her show tonight. Yes, she'd missed a couple of cues and fumbled over her costume and bolted from stage at the end leaving their MC Charlie, The Gloved Gatsby, to cover up with some clever jokes. Yolande was nowhere to be seen, so Reiko slipped out while everyone was congratulating each other on a good night. She knocked gently on the dressing room door.

"Yeah?"

"Can I come in?"

"Sure." Yolande's sigh filled the air as Reiko pushed the door open.

"Are you okay?" Reiko knew the answer was no before she even asked the question, but there was no other way to begin.

Yolande blinked once, her dark brown eyes filled with the sheen of unspilled tears. "Not really."

"I'm so sorry to hear about Helen."

"Thanks."

"Is there anything I can do?"

Yolande frowned. "Yeah. Have you seen my blue lace agate crystal? I've searched everywhere."

"No, sorry."

"My show was a total disaster without it."

"It wasn't a total disaster." Only a series of small hiccups, ones that were covered up by the really good team who worked the stage.

"Reiko. You've seen enough burlesque to know a disaster when you see one. Don't try to smooth this over. I've lost my lover, my dance partner, and my lucky crystal tonight. I couldn't cope if you lied to me as well."

Reiko nodded slowly. "Obviously, it wasn't your best performance, but I'm being honest when I say it wasn't a disaster. Remember that time Sassy Pearl threw up on the pianist? That was a disaster."

Yolande laughed, then pinched her lips together. "Oh my God. Poor girl. She got so drunk before her first performance and it all went wrong."

"And you know what? Even that wasn't a disaster. Charlie did a wonderful job in making the crowd empathise with her, the show went on, and the piano was eventually cleaned. We're all here for you, Yolande."

"Thank you." Her shaky sigh filled the air. "That does help."

"Anytime. Do you want to come and join the others for a drink? We've had a great night and Beth wants to celebrate."

"No. I might head home."

"Are you sure you'll be alright?" Reiko thought Yolande shared a flat with Helen. "Friends don't let friends hurt alone."

Yolande jumped up and wrapped Reiko in a hug without any warning, so Reiko had no time to prepare herself for the sensory onslaught. Heat flushed across her skin, and she breathed out slowly to steady her heart. The hug meant nothing. Well, nothing like she wanted it to mean, anyway.

"Thanks for thinking of me. You are a good friend. Maybe one drink. Come on." Yolande sprang away as fast as she'd hugged Reiko and if it wasn't for the flash of emotion on her face, it would have been easy to assume that everything was as fine as Yolande obviously wanted it to be. Burlesque dancers were fantastic actors, and the way Yolande easily fell into her role as the life of the party annoyed Reiko. Annoyed? No, it really bugged her. She was worried for Yolande.

"Are you coming?" Yolande poked her head back inside the dressing room, and Reiko nodded.

"Yes, of course." It took Reiko a while to recentre herself—especially after the hug—before she walked the short distance back to the bar. The crew at Seraph's loved a good hug and it'd taken Reiko a while to get accustomed to it coming from a non-demonstrative family. Now she loved it, the quiet comfort of a body pressed against her without the confusion of desire. She could even hug Yolande like that if she had a moment to prepare herself. Everyone here was so loving and friendly, and she needed them more than anything else. The sounds of everyone's conversation flowed around her like a warm blanket in winter, and she popped behind the bar to pour herself a glass of rosé.

"I can't believe she just left like that." Charlie had been the one to introduce Helen to Yolande. Charlie always believed the best in people, so it wasn't a surprise that Charlie wouldn't believe that Helen was capable of being selfish and hurtful. Reiko breathed in deep—it was a good way to live life, as if people were genuine—and given Charlie's background, it had to be a deliberate choice.

Yolande shrugged. "I only know what you guys know. I arrived here tonight and Beth told me Helen had called to say she wasn't going to dance anymore. She was sorry to leave Beth in the lurch but that was it." The unsaid comment that Helen hadn't had the guts to talk to Yolande directly could be read on everyone's faces, from Jack's wide eyes, Ace's sneer, and Beth's frown.

"She just ghosted you?" Charlie asked.

Reiko cleared her throat. "Technically it's not ghosting if she called Beth."

"Reiko. I don't think technicalities are going to help right now." Ace laughed, and Reiko tried not to cringe at the notion. She hadn't meant to make a joke if it might hurt Yolande.

"Yeah. It's a crappy thing to do either way."

"I think we all agree on that." Beth coughed. "I have some other news to share and it's not great. I wanted to wait until after the show to share with everyone."

Almost everyone groaned in a collective worried noise that echoed around the empty room. The phonics in there were designed for a crowd, not for a few mates standing at the bar chatting after a show.

"Get on with it then." Yolande gulped down the rest of her drink and squared her shoulders. "You may as well tell everyone. It'll stop me having to tell it over and over again." There was more in the Helen situation? Reiko wanted to wrap Yolande up in a blanket and make it all go away.

"I figured that you'd want that. And this news, well, it's going to need us all to stick together."

"To Seraph's. Our family." Ace and Jack lifted their glasses up high. Reiko quietly refilled Yolande's glass and smiled when Yolande gave her a little nod of thanks.

"Okay. News time. Helen didn't just quit working for us. She's given up burlesque forever because…" Beth rolled her fingers on the bar like a fake drum roll.

"Oh come on," Yolande grumped.

"Helen is getting married and we are all invited to the wedding." Beth announced this as if it wouldn't completely devastate Yolande. Reiko rushed around the bar and wrapped her arms around Yolande's waist. She rested her head between Yolande's shoulder blades, but it didn't last. Yolande pushed her away and bolted out of the room, leaving Reiko to stand there while her friends stared awkwardly at her. Now they all knew that she felt more for Yolande than friendship, and she'd been thoroughly rejected. She focused on trying to breathe.

"Helen can't be serious?" Reiko had to say something to clear the awful silence. Everyone talked at once, with all manner of horror and speculation at Helen's announcement.

"Why quit and then invite us to her wedding? And what is wrong with her that she couldn't give us more notice?" Ace's questions had everyone in agreement.

"It does seem like a dog act to leave so quickly. Perhaps inviting us to the wedding is her way of asking our forgiveness? After all, we don't know who she is marrying." Jack's voice of reason shut everyone up.

"Actually, I do. It's a Mr Blakeney. He's a stockbroker and third son of the Earl of Gattingly."

Reiko didn't want to hear anymore; Helen had obviously given up her burlesque family for a much grander one and at what cost to those left behind? Let alone the consideration of what cost Helen might face too. Life with money wasn't always happy, not that anyone would believe Reiko if she said that. She'd heard all the jokes about how it was better to be miserable in a Porsche than unhappy on the streets and she was used to getting zero sympathy from the few people that she'd talked to about her biological family. It'd quickly taught her to keep quiet. Inoue was a common surname in Japan, so people didn't always connect her to the powerful media tycoon that was her father. She'd worked here at Seraph's for years without anyone knowing and she hoped to keep it that way. She ignored her friends and raced down the hallway to Yolande's dressing room, then tapped on the door.

"Go away." Yolande's quiet sobs weren't hidden by the door and Reiko ignored the request.

"I'm so sorry."

Yolande glared at her. "Why are you sorry? You didn't break my heart. You didn't sleep in my bed for two years, and dance with me in the most intimate ways, and then suddenly one day just walk away and get fucking married. Was she with the other person the whole time? Why didn't I know?"

"Helen is apparently getting married to Mr Blakeney. He's the son of an Earl."

"Of course he is. I could never compete with that."

Reiko nearly choked on her tongue. "You shouldn't have to compete for love. Yolande, we'll all support you whatever you decide." If only she believed her therapist's words when she parroted them for Yolande; even after all these years, she still tried to earn people's love by being what she thought they wanted her to be.

"Thanks. I think I just need some time to myself."

"Okay. Let me get you a rideshare home and I'll tell the others." Reiko might not ever tell anyone about her trust fund, but there was one benefit to having it. She could help a friend in need. She pulled out her phone and booked the ride, then followed Yolande outside and made sure she was safely in the car before heading back to the others.

2

Yolande's hand shook as she tried to slide her key into the front door of her flat. What a disaster of a night. From the moment she'd unpacked her bag and realised her blue lace agate crystal was missing, she'd had an ugly premonition that everything was about to go wrong. Her lucky crystal represented wisdom, kindness, and honesty. Helen had purchased it for her. Yolande dropped her key; Helen had told her the crystal would soothe her emotions, reduce stress, and aid communication. She'd believed her and every performance they'd done since she'd bought the crystal had been perfect until she believed she couldn't get on stage without rubbing the crystal first. Their whole show had been choreographed for two people, and it had been wrong and impossible to dance her part of their show using an empty chair where Helen used to sit in her top hat and tails.

Worst of all, now she had to step inside the flat she shared with Helen and confront her over this whole mess. With a deep breath, she managed to stop her hands shaking for long enough to pick up the key, get it into the lock, and twist it. Part of her hoped that she'd open the door and Helen would be lying on the couch with a proper excuse; perhaps she was ill and couldn't dance tonight. Anything that would make tonight seem more like a misplaced joke, and less like her life was falling apart.

As she stepped into the hallway, a weird prickle started to crawl down her spine. She flicked on the light and gasped. Someone had taken all their things from her lounge; the telly, the couch, the ugly painting on the wall that Helen's brother had created… Fucking hell. This nightmare was never going to end. Yolande managed to stagger towards the kitchen table and grab the piece of paper sitting in the middle of the table.

Yolande,

I can't fight with you anymore. Brian has offered me a future. Please come to the wedding and let's say goodbye as friends.

Helen.

Yolande collapsed on the floor. It wasn't enough for Helen to quit their dance, she also had to move out without notice at the exact same time Yolande was dancing, literally trying to keep their sought-after place on the programme at Seraph's Burlesque Club. Helen had gone out of her way to avoid a confrontation with Yolande, which hurt like the blazers, but the real kick in the teeth was the note. The note that blamed Yolande for this mess. No. It took two people to fight. For a second, Yolande almost held her head high, but it didn't last and the overwhelming grief and hurt surrounded her. Slowly she sank down until she sat on the floor with her head in her hands, the note crumpled up in her fist, sobbing, until her legs went numb and she forced herself to stretch out flat. Yolande had assumed their love was for forever. She never expected to be cast aside for a Brian Blakeney, son of a bloody Earl.

The numbness lasted for a fortnight. Yolande buried herself in extra shifts at the hospital, exhausting herself at work. But tonight she was due back at Seraph's with a new routine and costume. She sent a thoughtful quick thanks to Ace, aka the Costume God, and Jack who had helped remind her that she loved the classic styles of burlesque more than Helen's preferred neo styles. As much as it hurt to contemplate walking out on that stage alone, she wasn't going to let Helen's terrible decision destroy her joy of dancing. She loved the release of endorphins that came from performing and the comradery of her fellow dancers. The playfulness of burlesque contrasted with the often difficult emotions of her job as a surgical nurse, and every week she found herself anticipating the moment when she was about to walk onto stage to the applause of an audience that she could tease. Yes, she understood the psychology of it. The continual search for approval and acceptance were all satisfied when she danced, when she bared her body for random strangers. It was amazing how shaking her arse in front of a crowd made her feel so strong and loved and powerful.

For now, that would have to be enough for her. She could step onto that stage alone, without Helen dressed in her dapper suit; so hot with her huge tits outlined by the custom-made tuxedo. Instead she would perform alone.

Tonight, she would be a 1950s show girl with ridiculously long lashes and a full skirt that would billow out and show off her arse cheeks when she spun around. Ace was going to bring her a bright red wig to complete the outfit, and she'd had her brunette locks cut into a 1920s bob which would make it easier to tuck her hair under the wig.

She nodded to Seraph's security guard, Walter, as she walked up to the main door of the club and the Pacific Islander opened the door for her.

"Everything alright, Yolande?"

"Yes, thanks." By now, everyone would have heard the sorry tale about how she'd been dumped for the son of a bloody Earl.

"We're here for you." Walter was married to their bar manager, Steph. Yolande used to be one of the couples working here; her and Helen, Ace and Jack, and Walter and Steph. Now she was back in the singles crew with Charlie and Reiko. Reiko, whose gentle care had been the sole shining light in the last two weeks. She'd texted every day to make sure Yolande was okay until she'd started to anticipate it. Yes, the whole crew chatted in their group chat, but the messages from Reiko were so personal, like she truly cared for Yolande's wellbeing.

"Thanks, Walter." Everyone at Seraph's cared for her and her chest tightened. She couldn't stop dancing just because her partner—ex-partner—had stomped all over her heart as she'd abandoned her.

"Hey, Yolande. I'm so glad you could make it." Steph called out as soon as she walked into the bar. Yolande glanced around the room for Reiko, who was busily wiping down a table.

"Hi Steph. Reiko." She waved in Reiko's direction and was rewarded with a little wave in return. Why did that make her feel warmer?

"Can I ask you a question?" Steph came around the bar and walked towards Yolande.

"Sure."

"Beth and I were thinking you should change your stage name. Pinky Boom Boom has negative associations now and a fresh start might be really good for you."

Yolande held back a snarl at the idea that everyone was in her business deciding what was good for her.

"Never mind. It was just an idea." Steph backpedalled so quickly that Yolande realised her snarl must be written on her face and she blew out a long breath to try and be less rude.

"It's not the worst idea." She swallowed. Helen had picked the name for her, and she'd never really liked it. "Don't mind me. It's been a long couple of weeks." She waved her hand and Steph nodded. The relief that she didn't have to explain was palpable.

"No problems. Doors don't open for an hour, so take your time. Ace is due soon with your new costume."

Yolande almost chuckled; both at Steph and her own reaction. Everyone here was always in each other's business, and that's what made it family. "How about we wait till he gets here, and then we figure out a new name. You're right. Pinky Boom Boom never quite sat right with me."

Steph's grin warmed the whole room. "Cool. I'll let everyone know." Steph picked up her phone and sure enough Yolande's phone dinged with a notification from the group chat. All week, everyone had sent her cute animal photos and silly gifs.

"Hey and thanks for trying to cheer me up. I really appreciate it." She hadn't been able to answer them all, but just knowing everyone here cared had been enough; especially in the empty moments when she stood in her flat without Helen and without Helen's stuff. Soon she'd need a new flatmate to help with the rent, those extra shifts would only go so far to cover the difference that Helen used to pay. She almost snorted; Helen paid no rent, only helped out with groceries and the other expenses when she could. She'd been out of work for most of the pandemic, and Yolande had fallen into the routine of paying for everything until it was a habit that she hadn't noticed. Wow, when had Helen just stopped contributing? She swallowed, knowing that she'd never admit as much to her friends because she didn't need to hear anyone berate Helen. They didn't understand her background, and it would be unfair to Helen to mention it.

"That's what friends are for." Steph's easy smile helped. For the first time since the Helen disaster had struck, Yolande began to relax. She leaned against the bar with her purse dangling from her wrist.

"How are you holding up?" Steph leaned closer and whispered.

"Not that great, to be honest." Yolande's life had been ripped apart, like a giant plaster pulled from a cut and the ugly wounds underneath had been exposed. "I guess I always thought Helen and I agreed on our future. We were going to adopt a puppy together." Heat prickled behind her eyes. Another promise gone. Helen had been so excited about getting a puppy; a creature who could unconditionally love her. The chill on the back of her neck wouldn't go away. How hadn't she seen the subtle digs from Helen? She'd excused and ignored so much.

"You still could."

"It wouldn't be fair on the puppy. I work shifts, so the puppy would be home alone a lot of the time."

"Get two."

"Steph. I'd rather get a kitten. I'm more of a cat person anyway. Helen was the dog person." And now Helen would get a dog with Brian and be happy. Bitterness coated Yolande's tongue but it disappeared quickly as she realised she didn't actually want a puppy and she had just let Helen talk her into it. Thank fuck they hadn't actually bought the dog yet and she wasn't left with a dog to care for, because she would care for it for the rest of her life. An animal didn't deserve to be cast aside just because their relationship had been. Oh dear. A complex knot tightened in her chest; hurt at Helen's choice to leave, and a tiny whisper of relief that she could stop giving herself up to go along with Helen's needs.

"So get a couple of kittens. They'll keep each other entertained when you are at work, and it's better to keep cats indoors anyway."

"Are you getting a cat? I adore cats." Reiko pulled herself up onto the bar stool beside her.

"Do you have cats?"

"I wish. No pets are allowed in my building."

Yolande sighed. "One of the reasons we got our place was that the landlord was okay with us getting a dog one day." It was a ground floor apartment with a small dog-friendly park across the road.

"You are so lucky to have a pet-friendly landlord." Reiko's soft exhalation left a faint warmth on Yolande's arm.

"I am." Yolande was going to start doing things for herself from now on. No more agreeing with Helen and doing what Helen wanted to help keep the peace. "Guess what. I'm going to get myself two cats; one older rescue one and a kitten. First thing tomorrow morning." She could be selfish for a change and put her own wishes first. Chills ran down her spine; how long had she sacrificed her own opinions and choices to keep Helen happy? If Helen had stayed, would she eventually have become someone else? No. Yolande was a carer; she would always put the other person in a relationship first, but she hadn't realised how one-sided it had become. It didn't matter though. She'd do it all again because she loved Helen, deeply. Helen was a flawed person but so was everyone.

"Good for you. It's exciting to do something for yourself, and after this… drama, you deserve it." Steph continued slicing up lemons for tonight's cocktails.

"Hello everyone. I hear Yolande needs a new stage name." Jack walked into the room with his usual commanding presence.

"I do, but how about you drop the teacher voice?"

Jack placed his hand on his chest mockingly. "Teacher voice. I don't know what you mean." He winked, and only then did Yolande notice that Ace stood behind him with his arms filled with suit bags.

"Oh, is that Yolande's new costume? Can we see?" Steph's enthusiasm had everyone laughing.

"Patience." Reiko's whisper was almost imperceptible under the general laughter. "Isn't the point of burlesque to tease and anticipate? These guys. Always in a rush."

"What do you mean?" Yolande leaned closer to Reiko.

"Maybe you should be the first one to see the costume. It is yours, and everyone else can wait." A faint splash of colour washed over Reiko's cheeks.

"Or we can share because we are like one big family here."

"Like I said, the costume is yours. Do what you want." Reiko shrugged as if her original comment didn't matter to her.

"Come on Ace. Let's see it."

Ace laid the suit bags on a nearby table, then tapped his chin with his finger. "Actually I think Reiko is right. This one is special. It's your debut as a solo artist. Besides, you might want a few alterations."

"My first solo show happened two weeks ago."

"Yes, but you didn't choose that. This one is all yours." Jack spoke some good sense. "And anyway, Steph said in the group that you wanted a new name. New name, new look, everything points to your debut."

"What about Royale D'Arcy? I've always thought that would make a fun burlesque name," Steph said.

Jack's eyes sparkled. "Fanny Peters."

"Ambrosia Mist." Charlie's voice boomed through the sound system. She stood on stage with Ben, the IT specialist, setting up for the evening.

"Juicy Cummings." Ace's suggestion had everyone groaning or calling out Eww.

Yolande shook her head. "You guys are terrible. Pinky

Boom Boom was pretty bad, but it's better than Juicy Cummings."

"So you don't want something vaguely rude?" Steph asked.

"No. Not Blossom Pussy, or anything like that."

Steph drummed her fingers on the bar. "How about something classy like Chantal De Ville?"

"Or Sapphire Starr. You love crystals and stuff like that." Jack reminded her that she'd lost her lucky blue crystal on the night Helen quit and she cringed. "Okay, not that one then if your expression is anything to go by."

"I don't know. It's too hard. I mean, last time, I just let Helen pick because I went around and around in circles and couldn't find anything." Yolande closed her eyes for a moment. She wished she knew what she wanted, who she was when she wasn't in a duo with Helen.

"All of that is nonsense." Beth's sharp tone made Yolande's eyes open wide.

"It is?"

"Yes. If you want the perfect name that suits you, you need to think about your essence." Beth had danced as Queen Bee before she'd lost part of her leg in a car accident. The name suited her perfectly. She was the queen of Seraph's, more than just the owner, Beth ran the whole place and had created a supportive environment.

Yolande was more confused than before. "My what?"

"Your essence. Who do you want to be on stage? Dominating, demure, cheeky, fun, racy? Figure that out and you'll find your name." Beth shrugged one shoulder as if that solved everything.

Reiko nudged the edge of her hand with her pinky finger. "You are the life of the party."

"I don't bloody feel like it now."

"Maybe not," Reiko whispered. "But that's who you are on stage. You draw the attention. You are the candle in a dim room. Joy."

Yolande shook her head. "Nah. Really?"

"Your laugh cheers up the room." Reiko's earnest comment didn't align with how shit Yolande had felt since Helen had broken up with her and she almost spat out a fake laugh to prove her wrong.

"It's true. You have a wonderful laugh." Steph waved her knife in the air.

"Careful. That blade is sharp. I don't want to have to use my day job skills here. This is my escape from that."

Everyone laughed and she bowed. "Fine. Throw in making people laugh as a skill." It did feel good to make everyone laugh, and she wondered why it felt like it'd been so long since she'd achieved that.

"Giggles McGee," Charlie called out.

"Oh God, that's terrible. What about Cheeky Cheeks?" Ace's suggestion was worse and at least the others groaned in agreement. The suggestions thrown around became more raucous until Yolande held up her hand.

"What?" Reiko spoke louder than usual and it was pretty funny to see everyone stop their banter and turn towards her.

"Violet Joy." As soon as Yolande said it aloud, she knew it wasn't quite right. "Hmm, nah."

"I don't know. Maybe?" Steph was correct.

Beth cleared her throat. "Why Violet?"

"Oh, Yolande means violet flowers in Spanish, so it's really just my name." She'd been named after her Spanish father's mother, a notion she found ironic given her biological father had abandoned her and her mum almost straight after she'd been born.

"That works. What is Joy in Spanish?"

"Alegría." Yolande paused for a second. "Violet Alegría. I like it." Cheers surrounded her. She kicked off her shoes and clambered up onto the bar before bowing to everyone. "Meet Violet Alegría." The room exploded into wolf-whistles and cheers as she strutted along the bar in her socked feet. This was her place and these were her people.

3

Several weeks went by and Yolande slowly settled into her new life alone. She was busy at work, especially now vaccines had been rolled out, and elective surgeries were happening again. Her new stage name, Violet Alegría, worked perfectly for the new routines she had put together, and the audiences had applauded vigorously at her last show. Slowly, with each performance, she began to remember why she'd begun to dance burlesque, and having complete control over her look, her choreography, and her costumes added to the pleasure. Tease. Trace. Bump. Grind. Swing.

The pain of Helen's departure from her life started to ease and she'd replaced the missing furniture with a few cheap old pieces from the local charity second hand shop. She hadn't splashed out on anything special, because now she had two permanent house guests who left hair everywhere. Captain was a three-legged five year-old mega-fluffy Maine Coon cat that she'd fallen in love with at the rescue shelter. He was aloof and surly, although recently he'd allowed her to groom his long hair with a brush, purring loudly throughout. And then there was the kitten, a black and white short-haired cat of no pedigree with so much energy, she'd named him Bounce. They were both neutered and up to date on their vaccinations, so all she'd had to do was introduce them to her and her house.

Her phone dinged.

Reiko: Sorry if this reaches you while you are at work, but I'm in your neighbourhood and was wondering if it would be ok to visit?

Yolande grinned. *Yolande: Me or my cats?*

Reiko: Both of course. She added a blush emoji.

Yolande: Absolutely. Come by now. She added her address.

Reiko: Thanks. I'll be there in about 10

Yolande read the text again, then leaped into action. She scurried around her flat tidying up, plumping up cushions, with Bounce leaping around her feet. After a minute or two, she sat down, and Bounce jumped onto her lap.

"What am I doing?" She didn't need to tidy up for a friend to visit. Reiko would understand, surely. It wasn't filthy, there were no dirty dishes, or mess anywhere. The place was a little untidy, but since Helen had left, Yolande had spent too much time cleaning, needing to fill her time with something to do. She'd stashed all of Helen's other stuff into boxes and stacked them in the small bedroom that they'd used as an office. One day, she'd give them back to her, and until then, she could close the door and pretend they didn't exist. A two bedroom apartment was too big for one person and two cats, and she often felt like she rattled around the place a bit lost. Every time she thought about downsizing to a one-bedder, one of the cats would rub against her leg and the thought of trying to find a pet friendly landlord depressed her, so she just stayed here with her old difficult memories locked in a room. If that wasn't a metaphor for something, well…

A knock at the door interrupted her introspection, probably a good thing. She stood up, cradling Bounce in her arms, and went to open the door.

"Reiko. Quick, come in." Before Captain sees an escape route. Reiko slipped inside and pulled the door shut behind her so quickly that they ended up standing pressed against each other with Bounce squirming between them.

"I'm sorry." Yolande stepped backwards. Whenever she was lucky enough to get a quick hug from Reiko, she was reminded of their size difference. Reiko was medium height, although she always seemed petite, because Yolande was tall and slender. She had a typical dancer's body shape, with long legs, and only lacked decent-sized tits, not that anyone in the audience seemed to care when she released them from her costume and gave them a shake and shimmy.

"Who is this cutey?"

"Bounce. He's only six months old and so full of energy." Yolande adored the little kitten who crawled up her top and sat on her shoulder.

"Cheeky." Reiko reached up and tried to pick him up, but Bounce dug his claws into Yolande's shirt. "Fine. Stay with your Mum." Reiko stroked the kitten along his spine, as she grinned at Yolande. The room heated up and if they hadn't been alone, Yolande would've joked about having gone weeks without sex. Sex? What the fuck was she doing thinking about sex around Reiko? Reiko was her friend, nothing more. She'd never given any indication that she might feel something different than friendship.

"Would you like some tea, or something?" Yolande rushed back towards the kitchen and Bounce clung harder to her shirt, his claws sticking into her skin. The pinpricks of pain helped remind her that she had just come out of a shitty breakup and she didn't need to be lusting after a good friend. How did that even work anyway? She wanted to shake her brain and tell it to stop being ridiculous.

"I'm fine, thanks. I really just wanted to meet your cats." Reiko was so studious, clever, and always watching people. Occasionally, Yolande had caught Reiko staring at her with desire in her gaze, but each time, Reiko looked away quickly and Yolande was never certain of what she thought she'd seen. Probably wishful thinking; her ego could do with the boost of being wanted. For her to want Reiko to want her was a mess that she really shouldn't contemplate, or think about at all, really. She'd had enough mess for one lifetime with Helen. It did no one any good to invite more of that into her life, not that Reiko was messy, but they were friends. Friends. She cleared her throat and turned slowly around to see Reiko standing in her lounge.

"The fluffy one over there is Captain. He doesn't much like people."

"Poor Captain. I wonder who hurt you before you came here. You are safe in this place now," Reiko murmured to the cat, who surprised Yolande by stretching, then slowly walking in a large circle around Reiko.

"I think he's deciding about you."

"Perhaps." Reiko sat on the couch and leaned forward to whisper something in Captain's direction. The cat lifted his nose in the opposite direction, which made Reiko grin. "He doesn't want to be interested in me. What a sensible cat you are, Captain."

"You really love cats, don't you?"

Reiko sat up straighter. "I do. People make so many jokes about them. Cats aren't rude. People misunderstand them because they don't show their affection in the same needy way that dogs do."

"That's what I like about them. I like that I can go to work and know that they are independent enough to cope without me for hours."

"It's important. I always feel so sorry for dogs who are left alone all day." Reiko nailed the reason why Yolande had resisted Helen's continual attempt to get a puppy, and in the end, she'd been right, because she couldn't be certain Helen would've taken the dog with her. She loved dogs, almost as much as cats, however her job and life wouldn't be fair on a dog. While they'd been chatting, Captain had jumped up on the couch and was now sitting less than a foot away from Reiko, quietly watching her. Yolande wanted to giggle at the way Reiko's quiet manner had seduced grumpy old Captain into curiosity.

The post slot on the front door rattled.

"Excuse me." Yolande wandered out to check what the postie had put through her door. A crisp white envelope sat on the front mat, wider than the usual bills. As she picked it up, her fingers registered the thicker paper and her pulse started to quicken. Crap. She slowly opened it, pretending that she didn't want to rip the high quality paper, and slid out a piece of paper that was exactly what she didn't want to get.

You are cordially invited to the wedding of Helen Smith-Brown and Brian Blakeney.

She frowned, then shoved the invitation back in the envelope, walked back into the lounge, and threw it on the table. It was none of her business how Helen chose to represent herself; and if Brian was willing to put up with it, well, that wasn't her problem either. The only unsettling part was the niggling worry that she'd also let too many things slide under her radar when it came to Helen. Helen's happy-go-lucky charm was addictive and it wasn't until she wasn't in the same room as her that Yolande ever analysed the actual words Helen had said.

"Is there a problem?" Captain lay curled up on Reiko's lap, and she gently stroked the purring cat.

"Look at you two." Yolande forgot about the bloody invitation and just stared at the way Captain lay content on Reiko's lap. The aloof three-legged cat had obviously suffered some trauma before Yolande had adopted him from the rescue shelter and it had taken her a few weeks before he was comfortable being groomed by her. He loved having his long coat brushed, but he didn't typically stick around for cuddles afterwards.

"He likes me."

"Everyone likes you." Yolande rubbed her eyes. Reiko was always present at the bar. Everyone's friend, but no one's as well. Did anyone really know Reiko? She was so observant in an intellectual way, and yet she worked in a bar. Was it Yolande's imagination or did a frown flash across Reiko's face before she bent her head to pay more attention to Captain? Bounce wrapped his body around her own legs, and she leaned over to pick him up.

"Are you missing all the attention, little fella?"

After a long comfortable silence, Reiko glanced up. "What was in the mail that made you so unhappy?"

"It's the invitation to Helen's wedding."

"Oh. I didn't think she'd go through with inviting us all. She seemed so keen to dump the whole scene and move on to her new life."

Yolande frowned. "She dumped me."

"Romantically, yes. But she also quit Seraph's. We thought she was part of our family. Our friend." Reiko sighed and Captain wriggled in her lap. "It's okay Captain." She continued stroking the cat and he went back to purring. "I know it's not the same thing, but she still hurt all of us too, just in a different way."

"I didn't even consider that. Does that make me a bad friend?"

Reiko's eyes widened. "Absolutely not. You've been badly hurt, it's okay to only have the space to think about your own needs for a while. We are all here for you."

"Would you like to be my plus one at the wedding?" Yolande blurted, and then held her breath because she hadn't really meant to offer that and didn't know why she had. Her stomach churned and she plonked herself down in a chair.

"Assuming Helen doesn't invite the rest of the Seraph crew, sure, I'd love to come along and support you."

"As a friend." Why did she need to remind Reiko of that? No, it was herself that needed the reminder. This whole thing was confusing, and she felt like she'd lost control of her own mouth and thoughts. Just riding on instinct.

"Of course." Reiko bowed her head again to stare at Captain and Yolande wondered what she was thinking.

"Hey, thank you so much for dropping by. You've been the friend I really needed during this whole mess and I've loved getting your texts every day." Yolande's pulse skipped a beat as she admitted needing someone else, right as she was realising how much she'd let herself disappear into her relationship with Helen.

"It's nothing."

"It's really not nothing. Reiko, you are an excellent friend and I appreciate you."

Reiko's hand paused on Captain's ribcage and she slowly glanced up. "The crew at Seraph's saved me. I'll always be there for everyone when they need someone because you were all there for me when I needed it." The raw emotion in her voice hung in the air and Yolande's breath froze in her throat.

"Oh."

Reiko shrugged and gave all her attention back to Captain. Yolande wanted to ask a million questions but something in the way that Reiko shrank told her that she needed to be patient. Just when she thought she'd burst from waiting, Reiko gently shifted Captain off her lap and stood up.

"Thank you for introducing me to Captain and Bounce. They are adorable."

"Anytime. Are you alright?"

Reiko nodded vigorously. "Yes. I need to go now. I have a meeting."

"A meeting?"

"Yes. That's why I was near your place."

Yolande smiled. "And I thought you wanted to meet Captain and Bounce?"

"I did. I came here an hour early for my meeting just in case." Reiko had barely been here for ten minutes, let alone an hour.

"Just in case you were able to meet my cats?"

"Yes." Reiko brushed her hands down her jeans, drawing Yolande's attention to the way they clung to her slender legs. "I'm not weirdly stalking you or anything. My meeting is near here, and I knew your place was close by because I had your address in my phone from the other day when I put you in a rideshare to get you home after—"

Yolande sighed, filling the silence left by Reiko's pause. "—when I fucked up the dance and Charlie had to cover for me. I remember."

"Yeah, then."

"Why point it out? So what if you have my address?"

Reiko shrugged. "I only mentioned it so you wouldn't think that I hunted through your personal things, or did anything weird, to get it."

"I believe you."

"Thanks. Well, it's been great. Captain is lovely and Bounce looks like he's very fun for you." Reiko paced out of the lounge and by the time Yolande stood up to help Reiko, she heard the front door slam closed. Why was Reiko in such a hurry? Had she said something wrong? Probably, but she wasn't sure which comment had pushed Reiko to run away.

4

———

Three weeks later, Reiko hauled her suitcase up the front steps at Seraph's where Steph was waiting for her. Morning rush hour traffic clogged the street outside Seraph's and she checked her phone. No, she wasn't late. Good. She rested her suit bags filled with various gowns for the different wedding events over her case, then gave her rideshare driver five stars out of courtesy. It was automatic, and unless they did something totally awful, everyone got five stars from her. With a short breath, she prepared herself for the day. Today—in a few minutes—Yolande would collect her from Seraph's and they'd drive up to the Lake District to the wedding.

"I can't believe Helen didn't invite everyone like she promised." Steph stood on the front steps of Seraph's with her hands on her hips. "But whatever."

"Weddings are expensive. I'm sure she wanted to invite us all. We are a family and that must matter a little." Reiko had been disappointed to find out that Helen's vague promise hadn't eventuated, but the timing, only three months after Helen had left everyone, wasn't much time to put together a wedding of this scale. Reiko also had mixed emotions about being Yolande's plus one without the rest of the Seraph crew in attendance. She wanted everyone else there to shield her from being in such proximity with Yolande.

"I guess I'm just jealous." Steph chuckled. "I can't believe Yolande asked you to be her plus one."

Reiko swallowed, unsure what Steph meant by that. "Well, if the plan is to prove that Yolande is strong and beautiful without Helen, then her plus one needs to be someone single." If Reiko had more social ability, she might have rolled her eyes and made a self-deprecating joke about being the most single person she knew, but she couldn't pull that off without sounding bitter. Bitter, huh, hadn't she dealt with this years ago and come to terms with being single? She'd rather be single than in a relationship with someone who didn't appreciate her. If there was one thing she'd embedded early in her therapy journey, it was that she needed to love herself before she could love someone else. Steph laughed, and it took Reiko a second to realise that she hadn't actually joked aloud.

"What?"

"You are so right. If I'd gone, Helen would know Yolande needed a support person, a friend, but with you being single, there's the option that Helen will think Yolande has moved on. Yolande is lucky to have you by her side, Reiko. You are a good friend and this wedding is going to be tough for her. She'll need your support."

"And I'll do a good job?" Reiko was only sure of one thing; that Steph must have heard the insecurity making her voice shake. This wasn't a great plan. Aside from having read the wedding invitation in detail and being able to see the subtext; this wedding would throw her back into the world she'd grown up in. Fuck, she really hoped she didn't know anyone else in attendance. Surely, she wouldn't. Even she couldn't be so damned unlucky. Brian was the third son of the Earl of Gattingly—she'd looked him up online and he was a few years older than her—and she'd only gone to finishing school here in England for two memorable years before quitting that world and going to university. They shouldn't have any peers in common, so the odds that she'd meet anyone from school weren't that high. Likely, they'd all know her father, but she was well practiced in not telling anyone about that connection.

The much bigger cause of stress was the perception that she and Yolande would be seen as together together—not that anyone knew of her unrequited lust for Yolande. She would keep that secret for herself, especially in these circumstances. And now, Steph had made it real by saying it aloud. Reiko tried not to gulp. Anyway, what else was she going to do this weekend? Work behind the bar, then stare fruitlessly at her thesis until all the words blended together into mush.

"You will. You are the most supportive, least sarcastic of all of us."

Reiko cleared her throat. "Beth is supportive—" She paused while Steph gaped at her. "—And too busy to take a few days away from Seraph's. I know. Besides, Yolande needs a plus one who is the opposite of Helen to make this whole thing believable, and I'm the least like Helen of any of us." Helen was tall, elegant, fucking gorgeous with huge boobs, while Reiko was none of that, and more importantly, Reiko had none of the confident stage presence either. A quizzical look passed over Steph's face.

"Speaking of Yolande, isn't she late?"

Reiko shrugged. They had a five hour drive ahead of them to get to the Lake District and Brian's family home, Rutheringholme. Being the homestead of an Earl, it was likely to be one of those ancient historical moment type mansions with lawns and other things that the aristocracy used to show everyone else how important they were. Reiko stopped herself; she'd grown up in wealthy Japanese society and it was no different there. In any case, it didn't matter if Yolande was a little late, Reiko had built extra time into the schedule for the road trip to give Yolande a break every hour. Just as she was about to answer, a blue car pulled up into the valet spot out the front of Seraph's. It sounded terribly fancy to have a valet spot, but it was literally one parking space that Walter kept empty in the evenings if they had a special guest. Parking was at a premium in London and Seraph's lease only extended to the one car space. Yolande jumped out of the car, clad in jeans and a loose navy blue t-shirt.

"Hey, sorry I'm a bit late. It took me a while to get Captain into his box." She opened the passenger door and bent inside, giving Reiko a brilliant view of her jean-clad arse. The view rendered Reiko unable to breathe or move for a second before she dragged her eyes away with an internal eye-roll at herself. She might be Yolande's plus one for this wedding, but it was fake. Yolande didn't see her that way; never would because Reiko wasn't anything like the charming outgoing large-breasted Helen. She mentally slapped herself for obsessing over Helen's tits. It wasn't her style—playing the comparison game—and she reminded herself that it only mattered because Yolande's tastes didn't align with who Reiko was. The last place she wanted to be was on stage with all those eyeballs watching her, picking her apart for their own satisfaction. Yolande had fallen in love with Reiko's opposite; charming, beautiful Helen. If that was an indicator of type, Reiko wasn't close to Yolande's preferences.

And she had a good reason for not wanting the spotlight, having had plenty of that as a child, trying to live up to Father's impossible version of who he thought she ought to be. When she'd declared that she wanted to stay in England after finishing school and attend university here, he'd been thrilled because a law degree from Cambridge would be useful for his business. Hinata, her older brother, had studied law at Harvard and was already proving himself in executive roles for Inoue Media. For a brief moment, she'd enjoyed Father's approval, but it all came crashing down when she'd told him she was going to study social sciences. Mum had stepped in and of course they'd still funded her studies, because the only thing worse than having a queer daughter interested in useless topics was to have the stigma of being seen to abandon her. As Mum said, at least she was only a daughter and could be indulged in her academic choices because it was unlikely she would join the business once she married. Yes, the whole spiel continued to bother Reiko, hence why she'd kept studying so she had a reason to live with some distance between them. She'd left Cambridge at the end of her undergraduate degree, and now was enrolled at the University of London for her doctorate. One of the benefits of a PhD was that they took a long time, eight years on average, and she needed that time to work out what she wanted.

"Reiko."

"Huh?" She'd zoned out, lost in her miserable thoughts. "Did I miss something?"

"Ahh, yeah! It's time to go." Yolande waved towards the car, and Reiko realised that Steph carried two cat boxes. She picked up her luggage and the suit bags carrying her dresses for the various events described on the invitation. One bonus of growing up incredibly wealthy was that she knew exactly how to dress for an event like this and she had many different clothing options to pick between. After loading her things into the boot, she quickly trotted up the stairs to say goodbye to Captain and Bounce.

"You'll be fine, Captain. Yolande will be home soon. I'll look after her." The cat gave her a look that showed his disdain for her reassurance, given he was the one in the box and she was able to go wherever. She chuckled and stuck her fingers through the bars of the cat box to touch Captain. He nuzzled against her.

"I didn't pick you for a cat person." Steph said.

Yolande nudged Steph on the elbow. "One of Reiko's mysterious talents was to woo my grumpy cat."

"Hey, he just wanted someone to appreciate him." It was something everyone wanted; to be appreciated for themselves. She swallowed back a sigh—that wasn't a conversation she wanted to voice—and turned to walk down to Yolande's car.

"Thanks, Steph, for looking after these two rascals while we are away."

"It's cool. You should be thanking Beth, she let us keep

them in our flat." Steph and Walter lived in one of the flats above the club. "And if you really want to thank us, you'll take loads and loads of photos. I can't believe Helen dogged us and we didn't all get an invitation."

"Maybe she wanted to but couldn't. Weddings are expensive." Yolande parroted what Reiko had said earlier and a warm fussiness filled Reiko's chest. "We promise plenty of photos. Come on, Reiko, let's hit the road."

Reiko waved to Steph and the cats and went through the motions of getting in the car and putting on her seatbelt. Yolande opened the driver's window and shouted another goodbye, this time with a wave and she even blew a kiss to Steph which seemed excessive, but also terribly like Yolande. Reiko managed a little wave; she'd never be as demonstrative as anyone else. For years she'd thought it was just habit, but on reflection with her therapist, she'd come to realise that her upbringing had given her the tools to be herself in social situations. She could fall back on good manners when she was uncomfortable with revealing too much of herself and it was actually okay to do that. Being an introvert was valid.

"Selfie time." Yolande held up her phone and leaned towards Reiko who smiled tentatively at the camera. As soon as Yolande put her phone away and turned on the engine, Reiko remembered to breathe. She was really doing this; going to a wedding as Yolande's plus one and risking Yolande discovering who her family was. It took a couple of breaths to calm the catastrophic overthinking that her whole life was about to come crumbling down. It wasn't. She'd deal with whatever happened and she'd be okay.

"You can put on whatever music you want." Yolande glanced over her shoulder, then eased the car out into traffic.

"If you plug in your phone, it'll connect to the car and play whatever playlist you select."

"Okay." Reiko did as she was asked and scrolled through her music app. "Upbeat?"

"Yeah. Road trip music."

"What do you mean?" Reiko could feel Yolande's stare, or at least the sense of it, even though she kept her gaze on the road. Had she somehow revealed something about herself without knowing it?

"Road trip music, the name kind of says it all."

"So… Songs about roads and travelling?"

Yolande elbowed her and laughed. "Seriously. You don't know what road trip music is?"

"No." Should she know that?

"Wow, okay. Um, road trip music is what you listen to on a road trip. You know, singalong stuff to keep you entertained while you drive."

"I don't sing." And she'd never done this before, had no idea that driving with a friend to a place even had a name. She'd lived in England for a long time and thought she had a good handle on most cultural stuff here.

"It's not a test, Reiko. I'm not going to make you sing. Just put on some music you like, anything, as long as it's not going to make us sleepy and restful."

Reiko sighed. She could probably manage that. Who knew that music was such a contentious topic? She selected a playlist and hit play and the bass of Cardi B's Up thumped into the car. Yolande laughed and started to rap along with the song, as she navigated London's traffic. It took many songs to get out of London and onto the motorway that would take them north to the Lake District.

"Thank you so much for coming along with me to this." Yolande's voice was low under the music and Reiko turned the volume down.

"It's no problem."

"I don't know." A fluttery note trembled in Yolande's voice, hinting at a sudden lack of confidence. Of course, she was going to watch her ex get married, and only a few months after they'd broken up in such an awkward way.

"You don't want to go? We can go home again." Reiko could avoid all that social interaction, especially the risk of meeting people who knew of her and her family.

"No. I think I need to do this. I need to prove that she didn't hurt me—"

"But she did."

"Yeah." Yolande sighed deeply. "She did, but I want to prove to her and myself that I'm happy for her choice and it didn't hurt so much that I'd avoid the whole thing. I'm not going to be a coward and treat her like she treated me."

"Okay. Makes sense." It didn't really, although Reiko completely understood the concept of wanting to stand up for oneself as a show of strength under the weight of hurt. She'd done that when she'd moved out of home, and she kept doing it every time she had an email or phone call from Mum requesting her presence at a family function. The pandemic had made it hard to travel—even for those with private jets—and it'd given Reiko a bit of space to work out what she wanted without her parents always demanding her time. She knew she was lucky to have the funds behind her that she hadn't needed to stress about money during the worst of the lockdowns; and she felt additionally fortunate to have a little time to think about herself.

Yolande laughed bitterly. "Does it? I wish it made sense. It all happened so quickly. I haven't had time to figure out how I feel apart from feeling like I've been pushed down a hill and I'm all bruised everywhere."

Reiko wanted to touch Yolande—hug her or rub her shoulder—to reassure her that she'd be there for her, but she was driving and needed her concentration. "It sucks."

"It really does."

They listened to more music as the miles disappeared. There was one awkward question that had played on Reiko's mind since Yolande had asked her to be her plus one. Having Steph bring it up on the steps of Seraph's had increased Reiko's need for clarification. She cleared her throat.

"Can I ask a question?"

"Sure."

"Am I coming along as your friend, or do you want me to pretend to be your lover?" Reiko was a fool for agreeing to this. She'd never been good at pretence. An ironic laugh stuck in her throat; she didn't need to pretend to be in love with Yolande. She had been for years, always jealous of her relationship with Helen.

Yolande giggled. "Yes. Oh my fucking God. Being my fake lover would be perfect. The perfect scheme to show that she doesn't matter anymore."

Reiko nodded. "Okay, cool."

"Is that a problem?"

Reiko blinked back the sudden and unbidden heat in her eyes. What the hell was that emotion? "Not a problem. I just wanted to be clear before we arrive." It took a concerted effort to breathe out slowly, quietly, to ease the tension in her chest. Pretending to be Yolande's lover would be easy, but also impossible, because it would give her a taste of the reality she yearned for but couldn't have. Yolande didn't think of her that way. Never would.

"Clarity is always a good thing. I'm so glad you are coming along with me. I thought I was cool with going. I was going to prove to myself that I could be happy for Helen and that I didn't need her, but as we get closer, the whole thing seems like a bad decision."

Reiko did rest her hand on Yolande's knee this time. "If there's one thing I'm good at, it's being the support crew."

"And we all love you for it, Reiko." Yolande dropped her hand off the steering wheel and touched Reiko's hand for a moment, sending shards of heat up her arm. After a while, Reiko removed her hand and rubbed it with the other one. With Yolande's gaze on the road, she was able to hide her reaction to being touched by her.

"I need to pee. There's a little village up there. We can grab something to drink, and then maybe you can drive for a while."

Reiko closed her eyes. She'd been dreading this part. "I don't drive."

"Don't or can't?"

"I've never driven a car." With a muffled sigh, Reiko opened her eyes. She'd never needed to learn. Growing up, she'd always had a driver at her disposal, and then at Cambridge, she'd walked or used the bus. Now she was in London, there were enough public transport options that she'd never seen any reason to learn. And she had enough money to fly or take a rideshare car or whatever if she needed to go somewhere.

"Never?" Yolande flicked her head towards her, her eyes wide and unblinking.

"Please watch the road."

A whisper of a grin stretched Yolande's lips as she shifted her gaze back to the road. "I can't believe you can't drive."

"Plenty of people can't drive. It's not needed in London."

"But you haven't always been in London, have you?"

"No. I've never lived anywhere where a car was necessary, so I just never learned. I'm sorry."

"Why are you sorry?"

"Because you'll have to drive the whole way."

Yolande laughed. "That's cool. I don't really like other people driving my car anyway."

"But it's so far." Reiko was confused by the sudden switch. Why ask her to drive if she didn't want her to?

"We can take breaks. If I need a snooze, you'll just have to wait."

Reiko nodded. "I don't mind. I'm the kitty, remember." She fell back on her usual self-deprecating comment because it was easier than anything else. Habits could be useful. If only she didn't feel like she was disappointing Yolande…

5

———

Yolande wanted to make a joke about Reiko being the kitty of the establishment, but she pinched her lips together because it sounded far too sexy. It must be a consequence of their discussion about them being in a fake relationship for the wedding.

"I prefer support crew over kitty. Whoever decided that the person who collects discarded Burlesque costumes was called a kitty?" Could she pretend to be Reiko's lover for three days? And what kind of family was Helen marrying into if they could afford a three day wedding? Many of her friends with Indian heritage talked about weddings in their culture being a huge event that took place over a few days, but Yolande had never heard of a white person doing such a thing.

Reiko laughed, a rare genuine laugh and Yolande's pulse kicked up a notch. "It makes total sense. Burlesque is all about the tease, the anticipation of sex. Why wouldn't you call the support crew a name that also references sex?"

"You don't mind it."

Reiko shrugged. "It's better than 'the help' or 'girl' or 'maid'. Or… Never mind."

"Or what?"

"Or any of the racist crap people like to throw my way."

"That's awful. I'm so sorry."

"Yeah, like I said, never mind." Reiko's expression told her to leave it alone. What could she offer as a white person in this situation but a listening ear anyway?

"Sure." Yolande turned off the motorway and parked outside the village shop. "Want anything?"

"No, I'm fine, thanks."

"Come on." Yolande jumped out of the car and slammed the door. She loved this little city car; she'd bought it a couple of years ago when she'd been promoted to head surgical nurse. It was good to be taking it on a long road trip, mostly she drove from home to work and back. After waiting for Reiko to close the door, she locked the car, and walked into the shop. What was the bet that Reiko had no road trip food either? Perhaps they didn't do road trips in Japan. Yolande didn't know much about Reiko's life; both her childhood or her life away from Seraph's, except that she'd grown up in Japan. Yolande only knew that because Reiko had mentioned it once after chatting to some random patron one evening in Japanese. Well, no one at Seraph's really talked much about their life outside of the club. Most of them were there to escape real life for a while. She paid for the fuel, then asked the guy behind the counter if she could use the facilities. He pointed her in the right direction and she waved to Reiko before heading off to empty her bladder.

When she walked back into the shop, Reiko stood by the door waving.

"Do you need a longer rest or should we continue?"

"I still have to buy my stuff." She needed an energy drink and some snacks to keep her going.

"It's okay. I've already done that. I didn't know what type of drink you wanted, so I bought a few options." A touch of colour rose on Reiko's cheeks.

"You didn't have to do that. I'll get the next lot."

Reiko glanced at the paper bag filled in her hand. "Next lot?"

"Yeah. We are road tripping together, we share the costs."

Reiko nodded. "In that case, since you are already paid for the fuel, I will get all the food and drinks."

"That's fair." Yolande hesitated, unsure how to broach the subject of money. From all she knew about Reiko—a student who worked in Seraph's bar—it was unlikely that she had a lot of money to share the cost of the trip. The fuel would cost a lot more than a few snacks, but maybe if Reiko didn't drive, she wouldn't know that. Was it okay to essentially lie by omission to her friend to stop her feeling too bad about her lack of funds? Besides, if they were going to tally up the trip, Reiko was providing a lot of emotional support to Yolande that she would never be able to put a price on. It was going to be a lot easier to walk into her ex's wedding with her head held high knowing she had a supportive friend beside her.

The trip ended up taking more than five hours, because Reiko insisted that Yolande took plenty of breaks to rest along the way. They ate lunch at a small pub in a village that required a little detour from the motorway and the food was lovely. It was late-afternoon by the time they drove down the long driveway towards the wedding venue. Yolande had had too much caffeine and her left eyelid was twitching. The last thing she wanted to do was talk to Helen.

"What is that?" Awe at the incredible old mansion stole all of Yolande's words. She wanted to take photos of everything and share them with the Seraph's group. The impressive stone building shone in the bright afternoon light. It had everything; a fucking fountain with a huge driveway around it, a long lawn stretching out into the distance, and the house itself. England was filled with these amazing old houses, but the thing that made Yolande giddy was the idea that she was going to stay here. Her? Holy shit. A touch of grief pinged her heart as she imagined sharing this experience with her mum. Mum would've loved this.

"Just park out the front." Reiko's soft command broke through the unsteady wave of emotion threatening to overwhelm Yolande. Grief could be so inconvenient—difficult and complex—when it hit out of nowhere.

"Of the house?"

"Yes. A house like this will have staff who will unload your car and park it for you."

Yolande stopped the car and twisted to stare at Reiko. "How do you know this?"

Reiko only shrugged, unbuckled her seatbelt, and proceeded to leave the car and walk towards two white men in matching uniforms who stood on the front porch. They had a discussion, and one of the men walked towards the car. It seemed Reiko was correct, so Yolande jumped out of the car.

"How does this work?"

"Welcome to Rutheringholme. I assume you are here for the wedding?"

"Yes. Do you need to see my invitation?" Yolande had no clue about the protocol.

"No, that's fine. Mr George—" The man indicated the other man. "—will verify those details and give you a receipt for your car. If you ever need it, just show him the receipt and someone will bring it around for you."

Yolande nodded. "And our luggage?"

"We will bring it to your room."

"Oh, so like a very fancy hotel?" Yolande had obviously seen this type of thing in movies, she just didn't expect to be living it. For a brief second, she wondered how Helen was coping. She shook that off. Helen had chosen this over her, so she could bloody well cope without her.

"Yes, rather like that. Historically, the best hotels took their service etiquette from houses such as Rutheringholme."

"Cool. Thanks for being so helpful. I've never been anywhere like this and didn't know what to expect." Yolande hated this uncertainty.

The man smiled. "I understand. When I first got this job, the amount of etiquette to learn was overwhelming. If you have any questions, about anything, you can ask me, and I'll help you out."

"Oh, thank you so much." Her relief made her voice all breathy, and the man smiled, before he dismissed her with a nod, and she had nothing else to do but walk over to Reiko and Mr George.

"Yolande Cantor and Reiko Inoue." Reiko waited while Mr George checked them off a list, so Yolande waited too.

This wasn't exactly the type of thing she could brazen her way through, and besides, she'd had way too much coffee on the drive up here, so everything seemed to go far too slowly. Her toes tapped inside her shoes. Should she take them off before going inside?

"Excellent. I've put you in the east wing in the Peacock room. Your parents have already arrived and wanted me to pass on their message that they would like to meet you for a drink once you have refreshed yourself."

"My parents?" Yolande pressed the heel of her hand against her chest. "There must be a mistake."

"He means my parents." Reiko spoke slower than usual. All that caffeine had really messed with her sense of time.

"Oh!" Arriving here had been enough without the shock of having to explain that someone must be pretending to be her parents. She'd never known her biological father, and her mum had died in a car accident several years ago. Beth, who had lost her wife in a car accident many years before, had helped her through the months afterwards. Now Reiko, someone else from Seraph's, was helping her in a difficult situation. She was glad she hadn't given up burlesque when Helen had left.

"If you'd like to follow Mr Simms, he will show you to your room." Mr George didn't blink at her response, and Yolande oddly wondered if they included that neutral expression in their staff training. A tall Black man in the same uniform stood inside the hallway. How many staff did they have here?

"Welcome to Rutheringholme. Please come this way."

Yolande copied Reiko, trailing after her as she followed the man along a wide entrance room. The floor had black and white checked tiles, leading towards a huge staircase covered in burgundy carpet. The walls were painted in a bright yellow, a colour that would have overwhelmed the space, except everywhere Yolande looked there were paintings filling the walls, so the yellow only peeked out between them. She followed Mr Simms and Reiko up the gently sloping staircase as it wrapped around the edge of the entrance hall, past ancient artworks. She paused to stare at one; it was bigger than her, with an incredible scene of an armoured man on horseback charging towards an army. The date in the bottom corner said 1756. Fucking hell. What was this place? A home or a bloody museum. She gulped, then trotted up the rest of the stairs to catch up with Reiko and Mr Simms who were walking along an elegant hallway. Tiny tables were dotted infrequently along the long walls, and each held a vase filled with fresh blooms.

"This is the Peacock room." Mr Simms opened the door, and Yolande's laughter caught in her chest. The room was wallpapered with an incredible pattern; large peacocks dominated the room, all of them staring at the one bed in the middle of it. She blinked. Why hadn't she expected that?

"Thank you, Mr Simms." Reiko, at least, had the presence of mind to guide Yolande into the room by putting her arm around Yolande's waist. When she removed her arm to close the door, Yolande missed her touch. What was happening to her? She should not be starting to notice Reiko like that; they were friends, that was all. Friends who now had to share a bed for a couple of nights. She rubbed her eyes. Too much coffee and far too many competing emotions bubbled in her chest and suddenly the premise—

sharing a bed with Reiko—added a ridiculously absurd touch to the whole day.

"Fuck." Reiko paced across the room and stared out the window. The sunlight silhouetted her petite body and lust blossomed across Yolande's skin. She tore her attention away from Reiko, as she slowly realised what Reiko had said.

"What's the matter?"

Reiko spun around, her face shadowed by the light behind her. "You heard the butler. My parents are here, and they have requested my presence."

"I take it that's bad." Yolande pressed her fingers to the bridge of her nose, unable to begin to work out what was going on. First this house, then the bed, and now Reiko's parents were here. Huh! Reiko was so good at listening to everyone else at Seraph's. People adored her friendship because of her listening skills. Reiko didn't talk about herself much, if at all. Even the other day, when she'd dropped by to meet Captain and Bounce, she'd mentioned she had a meeting but no details.

Reiko snorted. "No, it's fine. I haven't seen them for ages, so it'll be nice to spend some time with Mum anyway. It's just that I like to prepare myself for seeing them."

"And?" There was a lot unsaid in Reiko's statement.

"And nothing."

"Okay. Why are they here at Helen's wedding? And… Never mind, it's not my business."

Reiko stepped away from the window, removing her face from the shadow and Yolande puzzled at the wry smile on her face. "I'm sure they are here for Brian's wedding. Most likely, they are acquainted with his father, Lord Gattingly."

"Hence why you knew where I should park, and why

you were so comfortable with the whole—" Yolande waved her hands helplessly. "—thing."

"Yes."

"Is your family rich then?" Yolande clapped her hand over her mouth. What a rude thing to ask!

"It depends on your definition of rich."

At that absurdity, Yolande cackled. "Only someone rich would say that."

"The view from this room is lovely. Come and have a look."

Yolande laughed even harder. "Okay. You've basically just proved my point by trying to deflect me."

Reiko twisted her ponytail. "Fine. Yes, Father runs a media business, and he has many wealthy contacts. It doesn't surprise me that he was invited to this event, as Lord Gattingly has obviously splashed out on the wedding of his third son. You can google him if you must. I need a shower." Reiko walked through a door, presumably into a bathroom.

Holy fuck. Yolande grabbed her phone and typed Reiko's name into the search engine app. The results only added to the way her stomach twisted. She was so embarrassed about all of this; from the way she'd offered to split the costs of their road trip with Reiko and had assumed Reiko wouldn't be able to afford to help out with fuel, to the way Mr George at the front door had ignored her to speak to Reiko about her parents, and the way Reiko walked in here to this ridiculously fancy house and been at ease with her surroundings. A soft knock on the door interrupted her reading. She opened it to see a different person in the same staff uniform.

"Where would you like your luggage?"

"Wherever you think is best." Yolande was completely

out of her depth, and with Reiko in the bathroom, she had no one to guide her. The staff person pulled a luggage trolley into the room and proceeded to hang Reiko's suit bags in a wardrobe. They left their suitcases on the floor beside the antique wooden wardrobe, bowed, and left. Yolande sat heavily in one of the brocaded chairs beside the window and flicked through her social media accounts. Anything to avoid thinking too hard about the topsy turvy situation she'd ended up in. Did anyone at Seraph's know about Reiko's family, or was it just her that was ignorant? Yolande stretched her shoulders before they tightened up too much from the drive here. She probably should take some photos of their room for the Seraph's team, but her head was too full to do anything. If she opened that app, she'd be far too tempted to ask if she was the only one who hadn't known about Reiko's parents, but if Reiko hadn't told anyone, it felt like the rudest invasion of her privacy to tell everyone else.

On the plus side, stressing about Reiko and all of this—she glanced around the room again—stopped her stressing about how she was going to react when she saw Helen tonight. Fuck. *Thanks a fucking lot, brain.* She jumped to her feet and started going through her warm up stretches, needing to use her body. Each stretch helped settle the rushing noise in her ears and the squirm in her belly by focusing on each muscle and tendon. Slowly, her pulse started to calm down and her brain stopped bugging her with nonsense.

"Hey, are you alright?" Reiko stood before her wrapped in a bright blue towel, exactly the same shade as the tail feathers on the peacocks who graced the walls of their room. Had they matched the towels to the wallpaper on purpose?

It would be so easy to tug on the towel where Reiko had knotted it between her breasts, and watch it fall to the ground.

Yolande's heart sped up again, and she shook her head. What was wrong with her? She shouldn't be lusting after her friend, even though she stood there with wet black hair hanging over her shoulder and her slender limbs all exposed with only a towel to hide the rest of her body. What was happening to her?

"Yes. I'm fine," she croaked and then cringed at the roughness in her voice. Damn it.

"Okay. I was thinking that I should say hello to my parents alone. I hope that's alright."

"It's perfectly fine. I wouldn't want to intrude on a family reunion."

Reiko laughed quietly, sending a rush of heat down Yolande's spine. "I think that's rather overstating it, but thanks." There was an awkward pause, one that Yolande wasn't sure how to fill. "Oh, good. Our luggage has arrived."

"Yes." She didn't know what else to say. Reiko wandered across the room and picked up her phone from a small table. She flicked through it, then nodded to herself.

"Okay, so we are due in the main ballroom for the welcome cocktail party at seven. Do you have a cocktail dress?"

"Yes." Yolande had read every single detail in the invitation until she knew it by heart, stressing over what to wear to each of the events. If only she'd known she could've asked Reiko. "What would you do if I didn't?"

Reiko shrugged. "The staff are always prepared. They'd find you something appropriate in your size."

"Like how?"

"It's their job to make sure all the guests are comfortable."

Yolande felt like she was meeting Reiko all over again. Their quiet kitty and bar worker was so comfortable in this environment, when it overwhelmed Yolande and she'd assumed—wrongly—that it would be worse for Reiko.

"I thought I might meet my parents soon, and then come back up here to get ready for the cocktail event. You look tired, so you should probably have a bath or a nap or something."

"A bath sounds amazing."

Reiko grinned. "Indulge yourself. I'll be back up in a couple of hours." She stood there, still wrapped in her towel, and Yolande realised that she was probably waiting for privacy.

"Okay. Maybe I'll start with a shower, then a nap. Good luck with your parents."

Reiko's grin turned into a snide laugh. "Thank you."

Yolande leaped to her feet and rushed into the bathroom before she did something silly, like reach out and taste Reiko's gorgeous mouth. She wanted to kiss away the hurt in her laugh. What was happening to her?

6

———

R eiko hadn't realised how much she'd missed her family during the travel restrictions of the pandemic until she saw her parents seated in the drawing room at Rutheringholme. During that time, she'd spoken to her mum on the phone every week, which wasn't too different to before the pandemic. It shocked her to see how much her father had aged so much in the past two years. Her torso tightened and filled with cold as he stood up, his hair white and thinner, and his face drawn with deep worry lines. Maybe they'd missed her too, or maybe the therapy she'd been doing helped her see them in a better light. As a child, they'd pushed her to be her best self. Being queer was something they didn't understand, and she realised that there was unresolved hurt on both sides. They hurt her when they refused to accept her bisexuality or even try to understand why it mattered to her, and she'd hurt them by defying their expectations for her. They hadn't understood why she needed to leave home and stay away from them.

"Reiko. You are looking well." Mum held her shoulders lightly and kissed each of her cheeks.

"Mum, Father. Hi."

"Once we heard from Lord Gattingly that you were on the guest list, of course we had to come." Mum waved at the chairs, then sat down, so Reiko sat too.

"Any excuse to see you again." Father sounded honest, with a hint that he might have missed her, and her heart sang with hope. Family love was so complicated and seeing Father like this focused her away from the way he'd hurt her and brought back all the reasons why his choices for her were his way of showing he cared. It would've been easy for him to cut her off, but he hadn't. He'd given her enough money to buy a house and live comfortably without having to worry about her safety or health; and he'd given her the skills to invest that money wisely so she could have the space to fill her life with what mattered to her. He'd never under-stand why she lived in a one bedroom apartment—the view was spectacular and she didn't need any more space—or why she was studying for a doctorate on a topic that was of zero use commercially. He certainly would never understand why she chose to work as the kitty in a burlesque club, hence she had always avoided mentioning it. Most of all, he'd never understand that she was in love with Yolande, not that she'd tell him that fact just yet. Or maybe ever.

"I'm so glad we could spend time together before the celebrations begin." Mum leaned over and hugged her tight, more demonstrative than she'd ever been before.

"Mum. It's so good to see you both again."

"When are you coming home?" Father asked.

"Don't ruin this by asking that. Reiko looks happy in her

choices, and if the pandemic taught us anything, it's that life is short, and we should let people be happy." Mum leaned back against the lush chair. One of the staff came over and they all ordered a drink. It was nearly five in the afternoon, and they had a whole three day wedding to endure.

Reiko waited until everyone was settled again. "Mum, what happened?" Something must have, for her to change her opinion on Reiko's life choices so abruptly, although she would never say that part aloud. They'd always had negative opinions on her decision to live in London and study such a fruitless topic. Obviously studying racism was important, and they'd never go as far to say otherwise, not when it impacted them as well, but they had often told her how she could use her intelligence for more useful—by which they meant commercial—endeavours. Let people be happy. She wanted to ask what they'd done with her parents.

"Do you remember Father's business partner, Mr Miura?"

"Yes. Of course, he was always visiting our house." Reiko sometimes wondered if Father had loved Mr Miura as more than a friend, but his reaction to her coming out had stripped her of that notion quickly.

"He caught Covid and died, and so did his wife. His son, Fuma, is still sick, months later. It's terrible."

"Yes, my good friend Yolande lost many colleagues too. She's a nurse, so her work was hit very hard." Her parents had to know she was here as a plus one with Yolande simply because they'd read the guest list. Father made it his business to know everything. His media empire was built on gossip, not that he would call it something so salacious.

"A dreadful, dreadful thing. And your Father has aged so

much with his friends being sick. We were so worried for you, especially when that aggressive Delta strain was announced."

Reiko nodded. "I know. You called every week." And when they didn't, she called them. Her parents weren't particularly elderly, only in their sixties, but with all the media continually talking about the elderly being high risk, the health of her parents had been a constant worry.

"It helped us realise that life is precious," Mum said.

Father patted her on the shoulder. "And we wanted to see you again."

"I'm glad you came." Reiko knew she'd never get an apology from him for the way he had treated her after she came out, but she'd take this moment as close enough. Her therapist would say she didn't have to forgive him. It was complicated, and perhaps she could learn to be okay with a nuanced middle ground where she didn't feel banished, nor was she fully accepted. Father was obviously making an effort to include her in his life; he'd always given her enough material goods to mark her as his daughter but never really connected with her as a whole person. As he saw it, it was her choices that drove a wedge between them, not his reaction to her truth.

She relaxed back on the chair and listened to all their news. Her father could be incredibly engaging when he chose, and Mum was the consummate socialite, so they were very entertaining and an hour went past easily. When Father started telling her about how Hinata was doing well in the family business, and then began to hint again that it was time she came home to Japan to join him, Reiko stood up.

"I really must go and get ready for tonight's soiree. I'll see you then."

"And you'll introduce us to your… friend?" Mum's hesitation hurt like a pinch to the arm. Better than a kick to the stomach, and at least she was trying. Fuck. Reiko would need a few therapy sessions to unwrap all of this after the wedding.

"Yolande. Yes. I will." She bowed to her parents, then walked away with her head held high. It wasn't until she was out of their sight that she bolted back to the Peacock room. Moving quickly didn't do anything for the mixed emotions flooding her chest. How could it be so good to see her parents, and at the same time, a huge reminder of why she'd left home? There had to be a meme for that; good, good, bad, awful, great, or something. She pushed open the door to the Peacock room and clapped her hands over her eyes.

"Oh my god, I'm so sorry."

"For what?" Yolande asked. As if having Reiko walk in on her completely naked wasn't worthy of a mention or apology.

"For not knocking. You aren't dressed." She peeked through her fingers, keeping her hands over her eyes. Yolande scoffed as she slipped on a lacy g-string, one long leg at a time, and Reiko gripped her face tighter. Her fingers trembled and twitched, needing to touch those long legs, and the soft bare skin of Yolande's taut bottom. The g-string fitted perfectly, a sliver of lace between the round globes of Yolande's arse, and in another world—one where Reiko was someone different—she'd trace her fingers along the lace, all the way down over the bare skin until she followed the scrap of fabric between Yolande's legs.

"Seriously, Reiko. You've seen me mostly naked on stage every fortnight for how many years?" As if to further the point, Yolande turned around, her naked tits wobbling slightly. She reached over the chair beside her, grabbed a matching bra and began to put it on, apparently unconcerned about having Reiko in the room.

"A few." Reiko dropped her hands slowly and tried to ignore the intimacy of watching Yolande adjust her bra. The image of her bare tits was burned on her brain; she'd never seen Yolande's nipples before, so perfectly dusky rose against Yolande's tanned Spanish olive skin. Somehow being alone together made it worse. Her skin was on fire.

"Is that all? I'd venture you've seen me naked many times." Yolande shook out a black crushed velvet dress, then stepped into it. More heat grew in Reiko's belly, extending lower. She wanted to say, 'never completely naked', but her mouth couldn't move. Why was watching Yolande get dressed hotter than watching her slowly undress as she danced on stage? She breathed out slowly. Why, because this was real. It wasn't a performance. This was Yolande being herself.

"Can you zip this up?"

"Sure." Reiko managed to speak through the dryness in her throat. Her fingers trembled as she held the long zip at the base of Yolande's spine. The gaping fabric showed a little piece of lace at the top of her arse. Reiko bit her bottom lip, careful not to touch anything but the zip. Slowly she zipped it up, careful not to jag the fabric on the way. The dress went all the way up to a collared neckline and Reiko managed to do up the little button at the top of the zip without touching the skin on the back of Yolande's neck. Any touch now would cause her to combust, and from the little nervous sighs from Yolande, Reiko knew she needed to buckle up her own nerves.

"Ready to face the world?" she asked. Soon Yolande would see Helen for the first time since she'd walked away from their relationship and from Seraph's. Heat twisted and merged with a storming rage until Reiko couldn't breathe anymore. How dare Helen do this to Yolande? How dare she expect Yolande to walk in here, with her head held high and bless her marriage?

"No. I'm never going to be ready for this."

"I'm here for you."

Yolande spun around and pulled Reiko into a hug, so tight that she let out a squeak. If she'd been hot before, now her skin was volcanic. Fuck, fuck. She clenched her hands into fists, so she didn't caress Yolande or kiss her. Should she look up? No, that would put her lips within reach of Yolande's face. But if she stayed like this, it was just as awkward with her face pressed against Yolande's tits. Tits she'd seen only a moment before. Oh, she wasn't complaining—the opposite—but she lacked the ability to process this moment. Her pulse raced fast enough to power a rocket ship.

"Thank you." Yolande released her from the hug and stepped backwards. Reiko opened her mouth to speak, but nothing came out, so she just nodded. Thank fuck she was known as an introvert and Yolande wouldn't expect her to speak, because she couldn't. Her entire body was over-whelmed by being hugged by Yolande. Imagine how she'd be if they'd touched skin to skin. Oh shit, no, don't imagine that. She ripped her gaze away from Yolande. What now?

Get ready for tonight. Find a dress, put it on. On unsteady legs, she walked to the antique wardrobe and opened the door. With the door open, she could hide from Yolande and blink a few times, licking her dry lips until she was able to function. She closed the door again and turned slowly. Yolande's cocktail dress was lovely, crushed black velvet with a dog collar neckline, sleeveless, and slim line. It hugged her curves, all the way down to her knees with a small side split. Only someone with an incredible body could wear something so sexy and make it look classy, although a lot would come down to her hair and shoe choice.

"You are going to wear your hair up?" Relief filled Reiko's chest as she managed to speak in a mostly normal voice.

"Yes. Why? Is that bad?"

"No. I think it'll be classy with that dress. I was just thinking about what I might wear, since we are technically together."

Yolande frowned. "You have options?"

"Of course. I brought a classic little black dress, but since you are wearing one, I think I might wear the Valli pink." The choice would raise eyebrows as the theme for tonight was black and white formal cocktail wear, and her original plan had been to wear an antique Gucci ankle-length black gown with silver embroidery. She could wear that to the post-wedding function tomorrow night instead. Tonight, if she was to be Yolande's arm candy, the Valli pale pink dress would be a perfect match to her black velvet gown.

"Who are you and what did you do with Reiko?" Yolande put her hands on her hips and smirked at her.

"What?"

"I might wear the Valli pink," Yolande mimicked. "Less than one day in a fancy as fuck house and you've gone all weird and rich on me."

"Excuse me?"

"This…" Yolande waved her hands around the room. "This is all normal for you, isn't it?"

Reiko wanted to pretend she didn't know what Yolande meant and almost said, 'define normal', but Yolande was owed the truth especially given that Reiko had already told her to look up her family on the internet. Yolande must already know some of the truth, and tonight the reality of it would set in, when people fawned over Reiko's two thousand pound designer dress.

"Yes and no. Yes, I grew up with wealth and I have a trust fund, so I don't need to work. And no, this isn't normal for me. I choose not to live like this every day. I am happy doing my doctoral studies, which I happen to think are important—" She paused, pushing away the old bitterness at Father's reaction to her choice of study. "—and I adore working at Seraph's and being part of the crew."

"Even though you are only the kitty."

Reiko sighed. There was no 'even though' about it. "Because I am the kitty. Being useful to others matters to me. I have the luxury of not needing to care about status symbols or money, and I like doing work that makes me feel useful and others feel cared for." Reiko had taken a long time, and a lot of therapy, to figure out why she liked working at Seraph's as the kitty. It was less about fading into the background where people didn't notice her and pick her apart for not belonging to their 'set', and more about doing things that helped others.

"And you can walk in here and belong."

Reiko shook her head. "Think of this experience like travelling to a country where you don't know the language. Everything is tricky, just buying bread becomes an exercise."

"But what if I mess up with the etiquette?"

"Why do you care what a bunch of rich snobs think of you? Why should their opinion about you matter more than your own? Most of their rules are designed to keep people out. It's bullshit."

"And I'm guessing that's why you left?"

Reiko grinned. "Yeah, that's some of it." That and not being able to fit Father's expectations.

"In that case, wear the dress that challenges them." Yolande's smirk grew into a proper grin until Reiko couldn't help but join her with a snort and a laugh. The Valli pink was light enough in colour to almost fit the black and white dress code for tonight, and colourful enough to annoy those who cared about etiquette.

7

———

For someone naturally chatty, Yolande hadn't really been able to speak a word for over an hour, not since Reiko had walked out of the bathroom wearing that dress. The pale pink fabric wrapped around her petite body, casually knotted above her right hip, giving the impression that anyone might pull the end of it and it would unravel. Yolande knew that wasn't the case, she'd literally helped Reiko zip it on, carefully trying not to touch her skin, but it didn't stop her imagining Reiko wrapped in a soft blanket ready to be cast aside just for her. They'd walked down the massive glorious staircase together, turning to follow the signs leading into the ballroom, both of them staring straight ahead. When they'd been announced to the room, Reiko had smiled, and so Yolande had done the same. For an hour, she'd sipped her champagne and followed Reiko around the room as she spoke to people who all knew more about Reiko than she did.

And now Yolande stood rigid beside Reiko as she introduced her to her parents, still unable to do more than nod when they spoke to her. She didn't want to open her mouth and give away her lowly upbringing with her accent. Worry about not belonging wasn't the only thing keeping her lips sealed. As she glanced over at Reiko—in that fabulous dress perfectly made for the occasion—all she could think about was how her mouth was perfectly made for kissing. She wanted to take Reiko by the hand and drag her away from this stifling room and sweep her from her feet. Lay her on that huge bed in the Peacock room and kiss her everywhere on her tidy body that she'd hidden for years. She wanted to unwrap her and keep her discovery all to herself.

"Yolande?" Reiko nudged her arm gently.

"Huh?"

"Father wanted to thank you for your service during the pandemic."

Her service? Oh, because she was a nurse. How much of the conversation had she missed while dreaming about Reiko's lips? Shit. "Thank you, Mr Inoue. Like all my colleagues, I was only doing my job."

"It is a worthy job to have done and I appreciate it. I'm also pleased that my Reiko has someone to support her, someone who is capable, and understands how to stay healthy." Was that a backhanded way of saying Mr Inoue thought Reiko incapable of looking after herself? She needed to say something quickly or they'd all think she was being low-key racist or unable to understand his accent or something, when really, she was stunned he would say that in front of Reiko.

"Thank you." Thank you? Shit. Now Reiko would assume she agreed with her father's ... whatever that was. "I couldn't have made it through the pandemic without Reiko's support." At least her vague comment was true, even if she let Mr Inoue assume the support had been more than just workmates.

"Enough about that, are you enjoying the party?" Mrs Inoue jumped into the awkward pause to rescue everyone.

"I am. This place is amazing."

"The ballroom is four hundred years old. I'm told the first Earl had the room built especially for a planned visit by King James in 1620. Unfortunately the king became ill around that time and died in 1625 without ever visiting Rutheringholme." Mrs Inoue's knowledge of history was a little intimidating as it showed how well she listened to the people around her.

Yolande nodded. "Well, it is spectacular. These old houses must cost a fortune to maintain." Oh dear God, could she stop sounding so provincial?

"I rather think that is the point of the design." Reiko cast a glance up at the huge vaulted ceiling.

"Excuse me?"

Reiko giggled beside her. "There is nothing the wealthy elite love more than to let others know how much they can afford to waste."

"Reiko." Mr Inoue's voice sharpened. "Where do you get such ideas? Not from me, and any decent business school would teach you the value of efficiency."

Reiko shrank at his criticism.

"I'm so sorry, Mr Inoue. Reiko and I need to go and say hello to Helen." Yolande waved vaguely in the direction of nowhere. She hadn't seen Helen all night and she … Huh. She blinked; she hadn't even thought about Helen since Reiko had donned that dress. Yolande placed her hand on

Reiko's arm and gave her a little shove to turn her away from her parents. They needed to walk away quickly before this became even weirder.

"Why are we rushing away?" Reiko whispered.

"Do they always speak so disrespectfully to you?" Yolande whispered at the same time.

"Um, what?"

"No, you go first." Yolande kept messing this up. It was like her brain couldn't keep up with the world around her.

"Why did you suddenly drag me away to talk to Helen when I can't see her anywhere?"

All the air emptied out of Yolande's lungs. "Are you serious? Did you hear the way your father talked to you?"

Reiko shrugged one shoulder. "He's always been like that."

"And you just let him?"

"Stop. Please. I don't need to be reminded of why I'm in therapy tonight. Can you just drop it?"

Yolande gulped. "Of course. I'm sorry." She dragged in a quick breath, sucking in air like a smoker desperate for a cigarette after a long haul flight. "We'd better say hi to Helen before your parents notice."

"Sure. Where is she?"

"No idea." Yolande rolled her eyes and Reiko giggled. The happy little noise sent a flutter through her body. For a moment, the whole fancy room disappeared, and it was just her and Reiko giggling together.

"Yolande. I'm so glad you could make it." Helen's voice —the first time she'd heard it since before they'd broken up —stole away the last fragment of her laughter.

"Thank you for inviting us." Reiko's society manners

saved Yolande from speaking. She closed her eyes for a moment and tried to pick up her stomach off the floor. How could she miss someone so much that it hurt, while also knowing that it could never be the same again? Helen had made it incredibly clear that she didn't want Yolande.

"I'd appreciate it if you didn't mention—" Helen leaned in closer and whispered. "—Seraph's or that I worked there."

"How exactly did we meet then?" It was another cut to Yolande's already bleeding heart. She clung to Reiko's elbow, fingers digging in too hard, but she was unable to let go.

"Brian thinks I'm a model. Maybe we met at a dance class?"

"You want me to lie?" Yolande vibrated with fury. After all the things they'd been through together, now this? What the fucking fuck?

"No. Just be vague. You are friends of mine. Obviously."

"Obviously. Such good friends that you left without saying goodbye." Reiko's quiet determination rang clearly even though she didn't raise her voice any louder than Helen's.

"I regret my actions."

"That's not an acceptable apology." Reiko's voice was precise and the air around her thickened as if it knew something was going to happen. *Sure, Yolande, what rot!* She just wished she'd been the one to say that.

"Who are you?" Helen looked down her nose at Reiko, whose left eyelid fluttered almost in a wink.

"You don't recognise me? I suppose you wouldn't. I'm no one of consequence."

"Yes." Helen glared. "And yet you dared to suggest I wasn't much of a friend."

Reiko raised one eyebrow slowly. "I'm here with Yolande. She told me what you did to her. I'm only saying what needs to be said."

"If you think I caused you harm, Yolande, why did you bother to come? Just to sneer at me and call me names?"

"No one is calling you names, Helen. Perhaps we came to wish you well, despite the way you treated the crew at…" Reiko paused and Helen's eyes widened just enough to give Yolande a petty thrill. Being in love with Helen had stopped her from seeing this side of her. How had she spent so much time with Helen and never noticed how obsessed she was with how people perceived her? She grimaced. She had noticed, she'd just ignored it because she didn't want to deal with it.

"At the dance class where you met Yolande," Reiko finished with the lie Helen wished them to tell, and it only made the tension thicker.

Yolande smiled at Reiko, deliberately cutting Helen with a shift of her shoulder. "No one would believe you took a dance class."

"No one needs to believe that. I'm here as your plus one, Yolande. Obviously it was you who took the dance class with Helen. Surely, there is some truth in that statement as you must have had some tuition during your lengthy time… dancing." The way Reiko toyed with the truth reminded Yolande of Mr Inoue's slippery language. An unexpected warmth surrounded Yolande. If only Reiko's father used that skill to support his daughter, not undermine her, because when it was used like this, it was wonderful.

"Yes, that's it." Helen latched onto Reiko's comment as if she'd been given a gift. "We did a dance class for fitness and became friends. I have so few friends to support me at this wedding. Mostly it is Brian's family and acquaintances."

"We've always been a family at Sera… at the dance academy. Of course we would come along to be here for you on this most special of days." Reiko laid it on thickly and Yolande could only stare in wonder. Where had Reiko been hiding this skill? There was no doubt—at least to Yolande—that Reiko had mentioned half of Seraph's name on purpose. She slowly released her fingers from Reiko's elbow; hopefully she hadn't left a bruise.

"Thank you so much." Helen blinked once at Reiko's almost mention of Seraph's but still didn't appear to recognise her. "Are you comfortable? Have you everything you need?"

"Yes. The staff at Rutheringholme have been excellent."

"Brian's father, Lord Gattingly, brought on extra staff from the village for the wedding. Can you believe it?" For the first time in this whole interaction, Helen almost sounded genuine. Overawed at being the central part of this incredible show.

"I can. It appears that no detail has been missed. The place looks glorious and Lord Gattingly has outdone himself with the guest list. I've seen several A-list actors, a good handful of politicians, and several billionaires," Reiko continued with her soft tone. "I must say that inviting the media mogul Mr Inoue was a particularly brilliant move. I assume Lord Gattingly wishes to get global publicity for your marriage, or at least for himself and the Gattingly family. It's very impressive, although Helen… May I call you Helen?… You have missed one detail that you might have used to your advantage."

Why could Yolande sense that Reiko was about to pounce? And how had she never seen this side of Helen? With every person that Reiko mentioned, Helen puffed up with her own self-importance, and it was so familiar—the way she responded to having her ego stroked—that Yolande couldn't help but feel foolish. Throughout their whole relationship, Yolande had bolstered Helen's ego, changing herself to please someone who was always looking for something more than Yolande could give. It wasn't her fault that Helen had left; she simply couldn't give Helen the life and attention she so obviously craved.

"I have?"

"Yes. But never mind that, it's only a minor thing. Easily overlooked." Reiko paused and Yolande had to pinch her lips together to stop herself bursting into laughter at the self-depreciating way she referred to herself right after mentioning how influential her own father was. "Tonight is all about celebrating you, Helen, and Brian."

As Yolande waited for the big reveal, her shoulders had tightened, and now, with Reiko's shift away from her hints, she felt them ease and the tension melt away.

"Just one question, Helen. Are you happy with him?" Yolande couldn't help herself. If Helen wasn't going to be with her, at least Helen could be happy with someone. Wasn't part of loving someone wanting them to live their best life, even if it wasn't with you?

"I am. He's offered me a step up in the world."

Ouch. Yolande cringed. "What does that make me? A stepping stone." If ever she questioned whether she'd truly loved Helen, it was now.

Helen frowned. "No. You know me, Yolande. I've always

been a hustler. I'm sorry if you feel like I used you. It's not true." Helen's non-apology was one of those backwards ones that showed she wasn't sorry at all. It was just lip-service to the mess she'd left behind. Yolande gulped; she hadn't seen their relationship like that until Helen said it, but damn if it wasn't true. She'd been enough for Helen when they'd met, but she'd also never have been enough for Helen's need to keep running and climbing away from her past.

"Brian swept me off my feet and I fell in love." The kicker was that Helen likely believed what she'd just said.

"And you thought it would be easier just to move out with no warning and leave me a note?"

"You know how I hate confrontation. My family, well, you know the whole story…"

Yolande sighed. "I do." Her heart clenched as she thought about Helen's upbringing, and yet, a little stubborn piece of her found it hard to care this time.

"I would love to meet your Brian." Yolande could be the better person here. Months ago, when Helen walked out of her life without looking backwards once, Yolande could never have imagined feeling sorry for Brian, yet she did. Helen had used her as a stepping stone, and it was obvious that she'd likely do the same again. Oddly, Yolande didn't hurt at this realisation. Instead, a strange heat grew in her chest. Interesting. It was no fun at all being the stepping stone that Helen trod on as she climbed her way out of her upbringing, and yet, she couldn't help but feel a little proud of Helen for chasing her own version of success. She was the type of person who would always be looking for more, never satisfied, but she was also doing well for herself with Brian, for however long that might last.

"You would?"

"Absolutely. We were friends for a long time, Helen, and I would be much happier if I could reassure myself that he deserves you." It was God's honest truth. Having Reiko beside her had given her the strength to truly see Helen and to set her free on her chosen path with all the best wishes she could honestly summon.

"Thank you. I know I wasn't the best to you. I thought I had to cut you all out of my life to be able to be with Brian, and I'm so glad you came today."

"If he asked you to do that, then I'm worried for you." Yolande's spine stiffened. That asshole.

"No, no. He didn't ask. But look around. I can't have people knowing what I used to do as a job. I've told Brian I was a model, but the pandemic made it hard to get work. He's been helping me out." If there was any proof that Helen knew how to use her assets to get ahead, this was it. Taking your clothes off to model fashion was acceptable. Taking them off to dance in the evenings wasn't. The line between burlesque and stripping was a thin one with many burlesque dancers being ex-strippers and vice versa. Yolande had done a little stripping herself to help pay her way through nursing college. It was laughable that modelling wasn't seen in the same light by society.

"I'm glad you are doing something positive for yourself, Helen. Just remember that the people you've left behind also have feelings. A little thanks wouldn't go amiss." Reiko sounded bored, detached, and yet, there was so much unsaid emotion in her phrasing that Yolande wanted to hold her hand and get her away from here.

"I don't need to take advice from you." Helen lifted her chin and walked off.

After a moment, Reiko chuckled. "She really missed a trick in not recognising me. She's so obsessed with her new life among this crowd. It would've done her a lot of favours to have Mr Inoue's daughter as a long term friend, someone she knew before she tried to fit into this crowd."

"I can't believe she didn't recognise you." Yolande shook her head. "Actually, no. I do believe it. You look spectacular in that dress, like you belong here, and nothing much like the Reiko from work."

"I'm still the same person. Clothes don't make the person."

"It's not just that. It's the way you talked with such confidence."

Reiko shrugged. "The confidence is always with me, it's just that at Seraph's no one asks for my opinion."

"They should."

"No. It's fine. I don't want people suddenly paying me attention. I'm happy to be me, not my father's daughter. Once people know that about me, they tend to change the way they act around me. I'd rather have basic honesty than people fawning over me just in case they'll get to meet Father."

"Oh, that makes a lot of sense. Have I been doing that?" Yolande hoped she hadn't. Reiko paused for just long enough to send a wave of cold doubt across the back of Yolande's neck.

"I have, haven't I?"

"No. I mean, you have looked at me differently since we

arrived here, but I don't believe that you are doing it to gain a favour from Father, not with the…"

"…He was so rude to you. I found meeting him quite distressing on your part." Yolande was no psychiatrist, but even she could see that Reiko favoured a quiet life without judgement because her father had such strong opinions of her and what she should be doing with her life.

"Thank you. I have a complicated relationship with him. Shall we get more champagne?" Reiko walked towards one of the uniformed staff who held a platter with flutes of champagne, leaving Yolande no option but to follow.

8

———

Reiko wanted to thank her Mum for teaching her how to get on in high society because there were so many conflicting feelings rolling in her gut right now, that having manners to lean on outwardly was the only way she wasn't a puddle of tears in the corner. Being here was the starkest reminder of why she needed to visit her therapist regularly. It'd taken her a while to find a therapist who saw Father's behaviour as emotional abuse and didn't just sneer at her for having rich people problems. Money didn't automatically grant people a healthy outlook on life. She took a flute of champagne off the platter of drinks offered by a staff member and nodded her thanks.

"I thought she loved me, and it turned out all that time together didn't mean as much to her. She was just playing, having fun with me until she found a more secure future." Yolande's hurt vibrated off her.

"Here, make sure you eat something, otherwise you'll feel dreadful tomorrow and both of us aren't going to survive the wedding if we are hung over." Reiko waved to one of the

79

staff who brought over a platter covered in tiny white ceramic spoons, each of them filled with a small dumpling. Yolande scoffed down three, not caring who saw, and Reiko wanted to laugh at the way she attacked the food vigorously. Another platter with dainty bruschetta covered in sliced tomato and fresh goat cheese was offered, and they both ate a few before the wait staff moved on. There were little fritters with salmon and chives, tiny pastries filled with different flavours, miniature folded fake newsprint with hot chips in them, and delicate prawn burgers the size of a Roman coin. Eventually, Yolande looked up at Reiko.

"Are people staring at us, standing here, scoffing our faces?"

"I doubt anyone has noticed." Reiko offered her a napkin. In her experience, people were too busy watching the ultra-rich or the famous to bother with noticing what someone like Yolande was doing. Usually Reiko hovered at the edges of these events, trying not to be seen, and it was slowly sinking in how easily she'd faced off with Helen. Being at events like this made her feel like she wasn't herself; she was some sort of parody of the little rich girl, showing off her trust fund and her snobby acquaintances while standing there in an exclusive designer dress that cost more than the staff would get paid. It was obscene and she wanted to go back to Seraph's where she could just be herself without all this packaging and stress.

"Good. Oh fucking hell, what a night. I can't believe Helen wants us to…" Yolande looked around, then whispered, "—lie, and you know…"

"Her choice to leave like that doesn't make you a bad person for wanting something different. It's okay to want to be loved by her. You need to forgive yourself as much as her." Reiko wasn't ready to admit—out loud—that she knew this because she'd been in love with Yolande for a long time. Unrequited love sucked.

Yolande patted her mouth with the napkin. "How do I do that?"

"Forgive her or yourself?

"Yeah?"

"I'm not sure." Reiko was no bloody expert on this; look at the way she'd slipped on her old mask tonight. So much for boundaries, and if she'd known this soiree would be like this, she wouldn't have come along. She'd assumed the third son of an Earl wouldn't get all this fanfare—and certainly wouldn't entice her own parents to leave Japan for it. She'd been prepared for perhaps seeing a few old finishing school pals but hadn't expected Lord Gattingly to go all out and invite half the aristocracy and the media, aka her father and his business rivals.

"My therapist says that forgiveness doesn't mean you forget the hurt. Remembering the pain is what stops you from making the same mistakes, however, you can let yourself be okay with your past."

"When did you get so wise? Have you always been like this?" Yolande sipped her champagne.

Reiko choked on a laugh. "Hell, no. It took a lot of therapy and listening to people a lot wiser than me to figure this out. And the truth is, I'm still working it out. I'm supposed to have boundaries with my father to protect myself. Well, you can see how good I am at that."

Yolande stroked one finger down her face and Reiko shivered at her touch. "Stop beating yourself up. Having met

Mr Inoue for a minute or two, it's obvious your father is accustomed to getting his own way, and your refusal to bend to his will matters."

"Yeah." Reiko wished that was true. Mostly she did bend; as a child she'd bent to his will so much that she wondered if she'd snap in half. When he'd sent her to finishing school in England, she'd gone because he'd told her to. He had sent her to England to perfect her English and spend time with the daughters of his clients. Once she'd arrived in England, she had finally had the space to breathe away from his expectations. It'd given her the strength to apply for Cambridge University and tell him that she wanted to stay in England; far enough from his reach, and more importantly, it was a place where she had enough space to work out who she was. Not that she had an answer for that question just yet.

"Oh Em Gee. Reiko Inoue. I haven't seen you in forever." A tall blonde woman wearing a classic Coco Chanel original black gown with a scooped neckline and a dropped waistline, in typical loose 1920s flapper style, beamed at her and Reiko tried to not blink as she tried to work out who she was. Her decolletage was adorned with an emerald necklace that had to be Regency era and worth millions, but even without the necklace and matching drop earrings, the perfection of her outfit gave away her position in society as someone of importance. Only someone with the right family and money could combine antique Chanel with such a heavy ancient necklace and make it work. Reiko was only surprised that she didn't have a long loop of pearls as well because they were in keeping with the era of the dress, although presumably that was the point of the necklace. To create a juxtaposition that combined two precious old objects and made something uniquely modern yet classy.

"Yes, it's been an age."

"And is that Valli that you are wearing? Oh I adore Valli's work, so inspirational. You look incredible in it. I love the choker too." Who was this woman? She had those blonde white woman model looks belonging to so many of her father's acquaintance's wives and daughters. It would come to her soon, surely.

"Thank you. The choker is Australian opals and yes, my gown is a Valli. From two seasons ago, unfortunately." Reiko had paired the soft pink Valli with a choker of Australian opals because their deep blues and blacks were dramatic against the folded fabric of the gown and matched her black hair. That the choker was a sarcastic nod to the black and white theme of the evening only added to the appeal.

"Oh I understand, darling. It's been so hard to travel, and I do hate buying fashion over the internet, don't you? It's so lucky that Valli and many other proper designers are so timeless. Who are you planning on wearing tomorrow?"

"I haven't decided yet." She'd packed a Valentino pant suit and a flowing gown by an up and coming young Japanese designer, Satoko RK. The gown was beautiful and she hadn't been able to resist bringing it. Now that she'd seen who was here, she was leaning towards wearing it. Satoko RK could do with the publicity of being worn at a society event like this.

"Neither have I. It's so difficult to get exactly the right look, isn't it?" Could this very pleasant woman please say something that would help her with figuring out her name? Damn it.

"It is."

"It's so great to see you again, Reiko. Remember that time we went to the Duke of Benburgh's ball. I still can't believe you convinced me to sneak out of school to go." Ah huh. Lady Anne Mulgrove. They'd kissed once, after that ball, when drunk. Technically, they were both completely shitfaced, to use the colloquial saying. Lady Mulgrove, Anne, probably didn't even remember the kiss; Reiko's first kiss. It'd been messy and awkward and drunk, and she'd been only seventeen.

"I'm fairly certain it wasn't my idea to sneak out."

Anne laughed. "You are correct. I can't believe that no one wanted to come with us. Bunch of cowards."

Reiko grinned. She'd been so worried that one of the other girls would tell tales on them for sneaking out, but none of them had. She'd made a pact with Anne that they'd take the fall for each other if they were caught. Luckily, it hadn't come to that—she'd let Anne drag her into some wild situations for the sole reason that she'd been desperate to jump out of her uptight childhood.

"Lady Mulgrove, I'd be so honoured to introduce you to my dear friend, Miss Yolande Cantor."

"Gosh, it must have been an age since we last saw each other. I've been married for a while now to the Duke of Ailsburgh." Seriously—that wrinkly old man? Reiko forced her face not to show any distaste, and she took the opportunity to bow, keeping her head low, just in case her expression showed her reaction.

"Your Grace."

"Oh, let's not stand on ceremony. Call me Anne, like you used to. I'm so sorry you couldn't come to the wedding;

I sent an invitation to your parents and they sent a very pretty apology on your behalf. Miss Cantor, it's a pleasure to meet you. Any friend of Reiko's is a friend of mine." Anne carried on talking while Reiko's ears rang with a buzzing irritation. Father had declined an invitation to the Duke of Ailsburgh's wedding on her behalf without informing her; had he listened to the school yard rumours that she was more than friends with Anne? She swallowed—the only thing that made sense was if the wedding was around the time that she came out to him. How bloody dare he?

"Thank you, Your Grace." Yolande's voice was subdued.

"It's so wonderful to be here to celebrate another wedding. I can't believe Brian discovered someone as gorgeous as his fiancé, although I suppose he does bring a rather large … wallet to the situation. I didn't realise you knew him at all."

"We don't. I've never met him." Reiko recovered enough to stay in the conversation and the moment; and sent a little thanks to her therapist who'd given her the tools to manage her pockets of rage against the way her family liked to pretend she wasn't queer.

"Oh? But…"

"I don't really run in these circles anymore, so I've never had the pleasure of his company. Yolande and I are actually friends with Helen, his fiancée."

Anne's sculptured eyebrows rose. "I didn't realise she had any connections."

"It's a slightly delicate situation. She took a dance class with Yolande, and we met that way. I've yet to introduce her to Father." Reiko let Anne, the Duchess of Ailsbury, assume Helen knew of Reiko's family fortune. Helen didn't deserve the courtesy. There were so many questions racing in Reiko's head that it didn't matter. Did Anne marry the old Duke because she wanted to or was it a way to keep herself safe in a world that didn't want to outwardly acknowledge queerness? Perhaps the Duke didn't care about Anne's sexuality, given that his first wife had given him plenty of heirs and spares, and now he gained a trophy Duchess who would be brilliant at showing his children how to get on in this world.

"What a small world."

"It really is."

Anne tipped her glass to Reiko, and she duly clinked hers against it. "To old antics between school friends. Come with me, and let's introduce Helen to some other people of importance. The poor girl must be feeling so left out, only knowing you two."

"Yes, I'm sure she'd love that." Reiko had hinted at her own background with Helen as a petty way of showing Yolande that Helen couldn't keep hurting her, but this plan of Anne's to introduce her around wasn't going to help with her own need to stay away from the more toxic parts of the wealthy cliques.

"It's fine." Yolande slipped her hand onto Reiko's elbow again. This time her grip was soft and soothing, an obvious gesture of sapphic support, and one that did nothing to ease the rolling in her gut. "I couldn't possibly say no to a duchess."

"Oh, you are a darling. I see what Reiko likes about you." Anne slowly undressed Yolande with her eyes and it took all of Reiko's control not to lash out in jealous confusion. When Anne stood beside Yolande and placed her hand on Yolande's other arm, Reiko stiffened. She wanted to bat her hand away, but she couldn't. Not with everyone watching, so she let Anne lead the two of them across the room with far too many eyes on the three of them.

"Brian, I can't believe you didn't tell me that your Helen knew Reiko Inoue." Anne scolded the brown haired man who stood stiffly in a crisp tuxedo beside Helen. Only a duchess could get away with such terrible manners, not even bothering with his courtesy title! Anne barged into their conversation and everyone deferred to her. It was both grotesque and bloody brilliant.

"Your Grace." Brian had the presence of mind to bow his head before he asked, "She does?" He turned to Helen, who had the presence of mind to copy Brian's little bow. "Helen, you didn't tell me you knew the Inoue family. I asked Lord Gattingly to invite him because if we could get photos into some of his magazines, then your modelling career would be…" Brian made a funny kissing noise, and Reiko tried not to laugh at the absurdity. Watching Helen try and figure out this puzzle without enough pieces should've given her satisfaction, but she liked Helen too much to let her flounder. She might be jealous of her relationship with Yolande, but at the heart of it, Helen had been a good dancer who had treated her well. Beth wouldn't have kept her on the schedule at Seraph's Burlesque Club if she'd been rude to the kitty. And one thing mattered more than her own feelings—Helen was part of the Seraph's family. They always helped each other and forgave each other when they fucked up. She would reach out now, and it would be up to Helen to take the gesture and be forgiven. Family, with all the complexity that came with it.

"Helen. Can we have a moment?" Reiko nodded to the

side, and walked away from the group, hoping that Helen would follow. There was a little alcove behind a huge column, and she waved Helen towards the quiet space.

"What?"

"I wasn't going to tell you this, particularly since you decided not to recognise me before, but I think it would be embarrassing for both of us if I didn't clear this up."

"What?"

"I'm Reiko from Seraph's."

"You? No, she's nobody and you obviously know who that lady is."

Reiko smiled. "That lady is the Duchess of Ailsbury, and we went to school together. You might know me as Reiko from Seraph's, but I'm also the only daughter of Mr Inoue who owns Inoue Media, one of the biggest media companies in the world. The reason why I work behind the bar at Seraph's is none of your business, but if Seraph's has taught me one thing it's that we are family and we help each other. I don't want any attention, so you are welcome to continue with your ruse that you met Yolande at that dance class, and you met me via Yolande. You can claim friendship with me if you wish, however, I would like to see you apologise… properly… to Yolande for the way you broke off your relationship with her. You hurt her and I—"

"What?" Helen stared at Reiko as if she'd sprouted a unicorn's horn and was running around the room shouting absurdities.

"I will not introduce you to my family—who can help your modelling career just as Brian suggested—until you apologise to Yolande." All the rest of the conversation was window dressing. This was the only important thing. Helen had screwed up—badly—and needed to make it right before Reiko would help her. Helen stood still for a moment, and Reiko let her figure it all out.

"You? You are from a rich family?"

"Yes. And I work in a bar for fun. Seriously, though, that's not your concern. Apologise to Yolande, so that she believes you, and I'll grant you all the connections you need to survive in this world." Reiko waited for Helen to decide what to do with this information.

"You'll help me? Why?"

"Because it's the right thing to do, Helen. You made a mistake in throwing everyone at Seraph's away, but you can make this right. I've spent my life in this world and I know it must be no fun trying to fit in with all these people."

Helen blinked. "It's not. They are such snobs. They look at me like they know."

"They do know. But if you are my friend, I can open doors." Reiko shrugged.

"You?"

"Helen. You really need to stop with this disbelieving nonsense. I'm gifting you a huge opportunity."

"Why?"

For Yolande. "It's none of your business, but if you understand any subtext, understand this. Her Grace, the Duchess of Ailsbury, who you insulted just now with your shallow bow and by not knowing who she is… Well, she owes me a favour. Should I bestow that on you?"

Helen's eyes widened even further, and Reiko knew she had her hooked. She cringed at her own phrasing; fuck, an evening among her peers and she was thinking like them again.

"Yes, please. These people stare at me like I'm nobody."

"You are nobody. You've come with nothing but a pair of assets—" Reiko flicked her gaze deliberately to Helen's breasts. "—And many of them are jealous that you've caught the son of an Earl, even if he's only a younger son. But if you know me, then they'll see you differently."

Helen breathed out with a desperate air. "And all I have to do is apologise to Yolande?"

"For dumping her, moving out, and leaving her to perform alone without warning. Yes. That's all."

"I've been a shit to her, haven't I?" Helen's eyes shimmered with unshed tears, and if Reiko didn't know her better, she'd call it acting, but she'd watched her dance for years at Seraph's and they were part of the same found family. Helen hid her feelings deep—protecting herself against the world—and almost nothing made her cry. She might have been artless, but Reiko believed Helen wouldn't have done it without believing she was trying not to hurt Yolande.

Reiko nodded. "I won't pretend to understand why you did what you did, but you have a chance to make it right, and to fit in with Brian's world. If I were you, I'd take this gift." Reiko turned quickly and walked away. The problem with being empathetic was that she wanted to stay and reassure Helen it would be fine, she would be fine in this world of sharks that she had chosen to be in, but she couldn't. She couldn't make everyone happy, and she'd already said too much. If Helen thought at all about someone other than herself—oof, that was an unfair thought—then she'd realise how much Reiko adored Yolande. Reiko brushed down her dress and walked back towards Yolande, only to see Anne flirting like crazy with her and Yolande batting her eyelids at the Duchess. Brian looked a little lost.

"Hi, sorry about that. It's been a while since I saw Helen and we had a little personal history to resolve."

"Oh, I didn't realise that she knew you?" Brian looked as confused as Helen.

"It's only a passing acquaintance. She met Yolande at a dance class, and then I met Helen through Yolande. Let's just say that I wanted to remind Helen not to step on my toes." Reiko tried not to grin as Anne's eyebrow raised up slowly.

"Friendships can be so complicated." Anne tilted her head slightly to one side, as she considered Reiko and Yolande. Reiko was fairly sure Anne already assumed she was sleeping with Yolande, and now she looked over at Helen with a considered glance. It wouldn't surprise Reiko if Helen and Anne had an affair at some point in the future; well… She swallowed a big sigh. It was none of her business if they decided to cheat on their husbands. None of her business at all.

"They really can. I hope my little tête-à-tête with Helen has cleared things up. It's old news really." Reiko shrugged. "I'm so sorry if it's impacted on your wonderful evening, Brian."

"No, it's fine really. You girls just sort that stuff out before tomorrow." Apparently he was going to choose boredom and ignorance over intrigue. Years ago, when Reiko had played these games, she would've found the whole thing terribly amusing. Now she was just exhausted by it all.

"Anne. It's been so good to see you again. I'm afraid I'm going to call it a night. Look after Helen for me. She's been my friend for a while, and I'd really appreciate it if you took her under your wings and showed her around. Yolande? Shall we?"

A frown flickered across Yolande's brow. "Yes?"

Reiko slid her hand onto Yolande's arm, once more pleased she'd spent too many years practicing this, and guided Yolande away. She turned and waggled her fingers. "Good night." And yes, she caught the little glint in Anne's eye, a smirk that said, *'I know why you are leaving, and I would too if I had someone so hot to bed.'* If only it were true and not just Reiko succeeding at convincing Anne that her fake relationship with Yolande was real.

Reiko waved to her parents as she tried not to rush through the room. She knew how to make an escape from a soiree like this and it was subtle and took a few detours along the way. A suave wave to an old friend, another pause to take a glass of champagne, then another deviation to place the flute on another waiter's tray, a zig and a zag, and soon, people didn't pay attention to her and Yolande. They were just another couple flitting through the room, chatting to people, and no one noticed their passage. It took only the smallest amount of pressure on Yolande's arm to guide her towards a door, and out of the room.

Once they were in the hallway, Reiko breathed out. "I think I'm done for the night."

"What happened in there?" Yolande grabbed Reiko by the shoulders. "That was some weird rich people shit."

"Shhh." Reiko glanced around but they were alone. "Besides, rich people shit just like everyone else."

"Reiko." Yolande barked out a laugh and elbowed her.

"You must know what I mean. You know a fucking Duchess and she's…"

"Shhh." Reiko pressed her fingers over Yolande's lips. It'd been a jest but once she touched her, she couldn't move again. Yolande stepped away and shook her head.

"Fuck. I need a drink." She ran her finger along the tight collar of her dress.

Reiko summoned some confidence. "Come on. Let's go to our room. There'll be something to drink there." She didn't wait for Yolande, couldn't linger so close to the ball-room for a moment longer, and strode up the stairs towards the Peacock room, hoping Yolande would follow.

"There will be a drink in our room?" Yolande asked.

"Yes. Most likely, or we can ring for something." Reiko paused on the stairs. She held the handrail and twisted around. Being a couple steps higher than Yolande put their faces on the level; at kissable height.

"Isn't this a private house?"

Reiko didn't understand the question. "Yes?"

"And you'll just ring for a drink, like in a hotel?"

"Sure. Hotel service was based on old houses like this, and for a wedding, they will go all out. Come." She ripped her gaze away from Yolande and kept walking up towards their room. Tomorrow she would overthink everything she'd said tonight and hate the way she'd behaved. Just like the rest of them. She'd played their games and proved she belonged, now she wanted to hide away. Why had she said yes to this? She pushed open the door to their room. Oh, shit. The disasters kept coming. Would she rather be downstairs pretending to be someone she wasn't? Or here with Yolande with only one bed for the night? She walked to the cabinet and poured herself a healthy whisky from the decanter there, then poured another one for Yolande.

"Here you go."

"Thank you." Yolande sat on the end of the bed and crossed her legs elegantly. If Reiko had any confidence, she'd say something, but she couldn't find her voice. Instead, she gulped the whisky and enjoyed the way it burned her throat. She'd already said too much tonight. Way too much. All it had taken was one flute of champagne and she'd fallen right back into the world she'd grown up in, playing the same political games, caught between wanting to punish Helen for what she'd done to Yolande and help her out because she was a friend. Trying to please everyone and ending unable to be herself. Whisky might be her only chance to shut up her brain and stop the cycle of beating herself up before it started. It was the best option in a bouquet of unhealthy choices, so she drank and listened to Yolande gush over the decorations and food and all the glamorous people. At least Yolande sounded like she'd enjoyed the evening.

9

Throughout the wedding, Yolande suffered. It wasn't the wedding, which was beautiful. As a bride, Helen stole the show with a stunning flowing ivory gown and a bejewelled bodice that showed off her figure to advantage. Acid painted the back of Yolande's throat, and she craved water, thinking she might vomit at any point in the ceremony. Was it too much whisky with Reiko last night? Or just the gut wrenching horror of watching her ex-lover marry another? Both, most likely. A bouquet of flowers had been delivered to their room this morning along with a handcrafted card filled with an apology from Helen. It was nicely done, and Reiko had given a nod of approval as she'd listened to Yolande read it out loud.

Reiko hadn't really spoken last night after they stepped back into the Peacock room after the cocktail party. She'd seemed drained by the whole evening and all that weirdness with the Duchess.

Oh God, what was she doing here? She was a nurse, surrounded by all this wealth and double talking. She didn't belong here. Every glance around the church only increased her sense of dislocation. Seeing Reiko disappear back into her quiet self didn't help either; had she done or said something wrong?

"I don't want to see another lily for months after this." Reiko's whisper was a soft breeze near her ear and for a second it chased away the rising nausea.

"But they are beautiful." The ancient red stone church on the edge of a lake was filled with lilies and with the soft light coming through stained-glass windows, it was like being in a fairy tale. One where she was the step-sister, tossed aside and ignored until she wanted to be the villain. The absurdity of being the villain in her own story kept the bile down. There were no villains here, only complicated people chasing their dreams. Just because her dreams didn't align with Helen's; well, that was something she was slowly coming to terms with. How long had she been kidding herself?

"And out of season. Can you imagine how much it cost them to fly those flowers in from the other side of the world? It's obscene. Even if they didn't fly them in, they would have to be greenhouse grown to get them to bloom so early." Reiko sat perfectly still, as if she hadn't whispered at all, or shown a weirdly precise knowledge of flowers. What kind of person knew when lilies bloomed, or that these ones were expensive? Rich people, and Reiko certainly demonstrated that she belonged here where everyone wore incredible clothes. The jewels on display were like something from a museum, best kept under bullet proof glass with weighing machines and other ridiculous security measures, not worn to a wedding in a remote church in the Lake District. Reiko wore a flowing pale yellow and green gown that shimmered and floated around her, giving her a nymph like aura, and the gold and emerald jewellery she wore matched the dress so perfectly, it was likely custom made. When she'd asked, Reiko had mentioned the gown was by a young Japanese designer called Satoko RK. She'd stored away the information even though it was useless to her; she wore an off the rack blue halter neck dress that fell in drapes to her mid-calf. It had cost her less than fifty pounds on sale. Hopefully no one would ask her who she was wearing because she'd end up saying something snarky like Tesco.

"Maybe, but they are also gorgeous." Yolande tried not to think too hard about it all. Helen had admitted she was a stepping stone into this world, and the audacity of the comment, coming after the way she'd just left without a word, made her already fragile stomach churn again. Finally, the ceremony was finished, and the bride and groom walked down the aisle. A buzz of conversation filled the air, gossip following the couple as they moved together towards the main doors.

"Let's get out of here." Yolande needed to find a toilet or a drink of water or some fresh air before she chucked up all over the person seated in front of her.

"Come on." Reiko stood up, holding Yolande's hand, and said several *Excuse Me*s as she guided her past the row of people seated on their pew, going the opposite way to everyone else, who were aiming for the centre aisle. "I'm so sorry. Please excuse me." It took barely any time before they stood at the side of the ancient church, and Reiko tugged her hand again. Yolande followed her away from the ceremony and out a little door at the side of the church.

"How did you know this was here?"

"I guessed. Most churches of this age have a side entrance." Reiko pushed open the door and they stepped out into fresh air. "Everyone else will follow the bride and groom out to the main steps."

The spring wind was fresh off the lake and exactly what Yolande needed. She breathed in deep, pressing one hand against her stomach.

"Are you unwell?"

"Someone gave me too much whisky last night."

"Someone?" Reiko winked. Being here, surrounded by her peers, brought out Reiko's cheeky side and Yolande couldn't help but wonder how Reiko would respond if she mentioned it. She seemed incredibly conflicted about her place in the world.

"You!" Yolande shook off her contemplation. She only had a vague memory of them helping each other out of their cocktail dresses and laughing as they dived under the covers. She was pretty sure they both fell asleep before they'd touched each other. Damn it, if she'd kissed Reiko, she wanted to remember it. "We didn't… last night?"

"Didn't what?"

"Kiss." Yolande whispered, hoping the wind would take the word away before anyone noticed her hot cheeks.

"No." Reiko stared out over the lake. Even the weather was perfect today with a bright blue sky scattered with fluffy white clouds, and the water shimmered with their reflections. Was it weird to feel jealous that Helen's wedding photos would be fucking perfect? At least Yolande understood that emotion. The rolling emotion as she gazed at Reiko's stiff spine made no sense at all.

"Good." Yolande cringed as Reiko turned and gave her an odd look before gazing back at the lake again. "I mean, good because we were both too drunk for consent, not good because I don't want to kiss you." Shit, shit. She was making this worse.

Reiko slowly turned around and held up one hand. "Wait. Does that mean you do want to kiss me?"

"Yes. You were glorious last night in that pink dress, defending me."

"So, it's a pity kiss?"

"No. I'm sorry. I'm making a mess of this." When she was with Helen, she hadn't noticed Reiko, and it had nothing to do with Reiko, only that Helen… Well, it wasn't true that Helen demanded all her attention; Yolande had freely given it to her. Now Helen had moved on and left her with space to contemplate their time together, Yolande recognised that she'd allowed herself to have her time, attention and energy taken by Helen. With time apart, Yolande had come to realise that she wanted something more balanced if she were to move on to a new relationship. Would Reiko be that person? Or was Yolande only desiring kisses because Reiko was so good at supporting her?

"Don't stress about it. Last night was difficult for me too."

"Because of your father?" Yolande hated the way he'd talked to her. It was so disrespectful, not that Reiko showed she'd noticed and at least she had family. Since her mum had died in that car accident, Yolande had been alone. Except she hadn't because Helen had moved in with her soon afterwards. Had she let her grief affect the way she'd fallen into their relationship?

She gulped, her stomach still churning. One thing was true, she'd been committed to their relationship, and she hadn't seen how she'd let herself get absorbed by the notion of changing herself to fit what Helen needed. Anyway, family was complicated and Reiko's feelings about it...

"Never mind. It's not my business."

Reiko shrugged and the silky fabric of her dress shifted over her spine, drawing attention to her slender body. "It's complicated. I don't want to play all these games, but maybe Father is correct. I'm wasting my life with my studies, just hiding away from the world."

Yolande's stomach settled a little. She hadn't overstepped by asking her question about Reiko's father and his treatment of her. Everything was confused by the lust simmering in Yolande's veins bubbled at the way Reiko moved. Clothes didn't make the person, yet Reiko all dressed up was something to behold. How had she not noticed Reiko's lovely body all this time? As a dancer, she noticed the way people moved, and Reiko was her friend, always there, always supportive. She should've noticed. Instead, she'd overlooked her, hadn't noticed her steadying presence. They were friends. When had that changed for Yolande? In the last couple of months Reiko had sent her a text every day to check up on her, and somewhere in that time, Yolande had started to notice Reiko in a way that transcended friendship. She didn't know what to do about it.

"Is it that you feel like you don't belong anywhere?" Her guess was a reflection on her own muddled wondering.

Reiko nodded, her expression grim. "Yes and no. Obviously I belong with this crowd, by the very nature of having gone to school with some of them and being a trust fund kid. I don't want to belong because I've done nothing to earn that space. Charity helps with that guilt." Reiko sighed. "The only place I'm truly content is when I'm working at Seraph's, but it's still not real. I'm still lying to everyone about who I am."

Trust Fund. Shit. The casual way Reiko tossed that out there really illustrated the gulf between their lives. Who was she to think about kissing someone like Reiko? There was an irony in it, since she'd had no qualms about being Helen's stepping stone into this world, not that she'd known it in so many words. The brutal truth had come later, and as she looked back over their relationship, she noticed the behaviour and habits. She'd supported Helen since she first arrived at Seraph's with the idea of a duo performance, helping Helen with her confidence, and they'd danced together for a few months before Yolande's mum had died. It was then that Helen had moved into her house. They'd become lovers almost right away; Yolande had been desperate to be held by someone. Helen adored being the one who Yolande turned to, and she adored the applause when they danced, needing the audience in a way that Yolande didn't. Yolande liked to dance, and burlesque gave her freedom and the thrill of playing with innuendo and anticipation. Ultimately, their needs from the audience were different—Helen needed their validation of her beauty and worth, while Yolande liked to tease everyone and enjoyed seeing them respond to her. Yolande knew she was a worthy person, battered temporarily by Helen's choice. So why did she feel inadequate beside Reiko? Money was a ridiculous reason to feel less than someone, especially when Reiko had created a life for herself where she wasn't part of this whole fiasco.

"Other people don't need to understand your choices. They are yours."

"True."

"Yesterday—" Hell, was it only yesterday? "—you talked about forgiving myself for the way Helen treated me. Well, you were right. Seeing Helen today, living her best life, makes me happy for her. Yes, she hurt me with the way she discarded me and that hurt will always be there, but it's a good reminder not to lose myself in a relationship again. I forgive her and I forgive myself."

"Brilliant." Reiko's smile shone with the same brilliance as the sun.

"And you need to do the same. It's okay to wonder about finding your own space, and maybe you'll forever be caught between two worlds, but from what I can see, you've done a really good job at finding ways to be yourself."

Reiko nodded. "Three worlds. I don't completely belong as an academic either." The sun glinted off the lake, creating a little halo of light around Reiko's body, with her dress glowing golden under the spring sunshine. She was a goddamn angel in this fairy tale picturesque view. Only a few steps separated them, and it was the easiest thing in the world for Yolande to close the space between them. She wrapped her arms around Reiko's waist, pulling her closer.

"Thank you for coming here with me." What she wanted to say was too awkward to put into words; that she was grateful for Reiko's support, that she finally saw Reiko, and she was sorry that it took her so long. But she couldn't say that without implying that it was the wealth, this odd society of rich people and how Reiko belonged to it, that had helped her see her better. She wanted to avoid that implication because it would hurt Reiko deeply.

She adored Reiko's careful smiles and her intelligent gaze, and the way she cared so much for everyone. Even Helen, who arguably didn't deserve her support, was still introduced to a Duchess by Reiko and given a chance to belong to the life she aspired to. Reiko didn't have to ask Helen to apologise, she didn't have to be kind, but she was. It was ingrained in her as core to her character. Yolande admired her very much.

"I'm glad you chose me as your plus one."

There was nothing else to do or say, so Yolande bent her head and kissed Reiko. She tasted like strawberry lipstick and mint, homely and friendly, like a fresh spring breeze that refreshed and smelled like hope and new growth. Yolande waited for Reiko, keeping her kiss light, uncertain if her advance was welcome, but when Reiko placed her hands on Yolande's elbows and pulled her closer, she knew. Perhaps it was too soon—only three months—after Helen threw her away, or perhaps the timing was fine. The answer to those questions could wait because her mouth was on Reiko's lips, and Reiko was kissing her in return. Reiko parted her lips, her tongue seeking out Yolande's own, until the kiss slowly grew from gentle to desperate. The satin of Reiko's dress slid under Yolande's hands as she deepened their connection. She wanted to touch Reiko everywhere, but they were outdoors, so she contented herself with a firm stroke up Reiko's spine until her fingers threaded into Reiko's soft hair.

"Careful."

"Oh?" Yolande lifted her head and stared.

"It took the hairdresser an hour to get my hair done." Reiko grinned.

"You care about that?" Yolande struggled to figure out what Reiko wasn't saying.

"I don't care about my hair, and I rather like the idea of looking all kiss-tussled, however, my parents are at this wedding."

"Shit. Right." Yolande jumped away from Reiko, her heart pounding. Reiko kept hold of her hands and squeezed gently.

"It's fine. I think I'm just—" She didn't finish, just looked away.

"You are what?" Had Yolande overstepped somehow?

Reiko shook her head gently. "I guess I can't believe that you want to kiss me. Me, the kitty who no one sees, while you are the brave, gorgeous dancer who gets the adoring audience."

"Don't undersell yourself. Dancers are interchangeable. A good kitty is irreplaceable." Yolande's stomach churned once more. She didn't understand any of this.

"Let's go back inside." Reiko waved dismissively; it felt like Reiko was leaping between conclusions and Yolande was missing key pieces of information. They'd gone from the wedding and hair to Reikos' parents knowing she'd been kissed to now wondering about her role at Seraph's. If Yolande hadn't spent so long getting her eye makeup just right, she'd rub her eyes right now.

"Inside?"

"We promised everyone photos, and they'll adore the way the church was decorated."

"I thought you were upset about the cost of the lilies?"

"I am. But just because I don't like them, doesn't mean I can't see how others can enjoy them."

Yolande shook her head, then followed Reiko back into the church and watched her take a bunch of different photos of the magical atmosphere. Something was wrong. A long silence hovered. Yolande stared blankly at the way the sunlight created colourful rainbows as it danced through the stained glass windows to work out what the problem was. She wanted to growl and kick something because she was doing it again. Throughout her entire relationship with Helen, she'd followed. She'd spent too long wondering what Helen was thinking and over-analysing everything until she gave in and just did whatever Helen wanted even when it made no sense to her.

Watching Reiko happily take photos to send to the team at Seraph's made her feel like she was about to willingly bash her head against that brick wall again. Here she was, in an environment where she was out of her depth, uncomfortable, and she felt like she was ignoring her own opinions in favour of Reiko's. She wasn't like this at work, where she was precise with her nursing equipment, and could run her station with confidence. Why couldn't she bring that same energy to a relationship?

"What's the matter?" Reiko slipped onto the pew next to her and held her hand.

"Just thinking."

"Overthinking?"

Yolande sighed. "What is the difference? I—"

"Just tell me, Yolande. We've been friends for a long time and I'm a good listener."

"I don't want you to feel that I kissed you just because of

your money." She growled. "Or because I'm overwhelmed by this bloody wedding and the way Helen just threw me away for all of this."

"Hey, you are allowed to have complicated feelings. This is a pretty fucked up situation."

"Yes." Yolande blew out a hard breath. "It really is. I wish my life was simpler, and we could just keep kissing." Her cheeks stung with heat.

"I would also like to keep kissing you." Reiko kept her face turned away, and when Yolande gently traced her finger along Reiko's jaw, she shivered. Yolande didn't move, just waited until Reiko slowly lifted her face and gazed at her with her gorgeous brown eyes.

"Your lipstick is all smudged." Yolande caressed Reiko's bottom lip with her thumb, still waiting, still holding her breath.

"It is?"

Yolande let out the air trapped in her lungs as she realised she was waiting for Reiko to kiss her; just like she used to do with Helen. It was time for her to stop following and to start doing what she wanted, to choreograph her own life and dance to the tune she picked. She'd started with her new routine at Seraph's and it was amazing to be a 1950s show girl instead of a modern neo-Burlesque dancer in bondage leather like Helen had preferred. It was time to take that same energy and apply it to kissing.

Reiko had already said she wanted more kissing, so the only thing stopping Yolande was her own hesitation, her own history of overstepping with Helen and getting in trouble. She vowed to break the habit. Right now. She leaned forward and kissed Reiko. There was no negative repercussion. Reiko kissed her right back and they kissed. They kissed and kissed, and it was perfect. It was equal and fun and delightful and like a homecoming. It was everything— their kiss.

A gentle cough echoed in the empty church and Reiko lifted her head slowly, leaving Yolande dazed.

"I'm so sorry to interrupt, but the last bus is about to leave." Mr Simms, who'd been so helpful when she'd arrived at Rutheringholme, stood in the aisle.

"Thank you. We will be right there." Reiko stood up with a little tug on Yolande's hands. The simple act of standing up and moving to the aisle gave Yolande time to find her sense of balance again. Her head spun in the aftermath of kissing Reiko; she wanted more. Needed more.

"We'd better get a selfie for our friends before we go." Reiko held up her phone and Yolande smiled at the screen. Her lipstick was all smudged and she had that post-kissing glow—everyone would know—but she didn't care. It was worth it. She wanted to declare to the world that she'd just enjoyed the best kisses of her life.

Mr Simms held out his hand. "I'll take your photo. You two are so cute."

Reiko handed him her phone and grinned. "Thank you."

"Over here. The light is best and it'll make your gown glow."

"Is that in your training?" Yolande blurted then closed her eyes. Shit. But Mr Simms just laughed.

"No. Photography is just my hobby."

"It's a useful hobby to have in your job." Could she just shush? Fucking hell, all those kisses with Reiko had stripped away her ability to talk with any sense. Well, nah, but she'd rather blame that than think too hard about how she didn't belong here and she had no clue how to speak in this circumstance. She was used to being the nurse, the staff member who is overlooked, not the guest who asked and got whatever they wanted.

Mr Simms's smile grew, and he winked at her. "Yes, there's nothing the rich love more than getting their photo taken."

"But only if it's a good photo." Reiko grinned. "Father has built his business on the notion that people love to look at good photos of themselves."

Mr Simms didn't blink at her comment, apparently accustomed to hearing stuff like that. "Come on. Over here."

They posed and he took a bunch of photos, and with each one, he joked. Yolande felt the tension in her shoulders relax with each jest. She wished she could figure out how to say something cute and funny without it sounding awkward as hell.

"Now kiss."

Yolande couldn't resist the order—this was something she could do well. She held Reiko firmly around the waist and tipped her backwards for a dramatic kiss.

"Yes, like that. Hold that, right there." Mr Simms rushed over and spread Reiko's gown out, and Yolande was glad she had great core strength from dancing as she waited. "Okay. Now."

She kissed Reiko like it was their first kiss; no, like it was their forever.

"You are going to love this one." Mr Simms waited until Yolande pulled Reiko upright, then handed her the phone.

"Thank you so much." Reiko flicked through her phone, with a brilliant smile on her beautiful face. "Oh I adore this one. You've really captured the light. Do you mind if I show it to Father?"

"Who?"

"My father, Mr Inoue from Inoue Media. He's always looking for quality imagery, and I'll make sure you get paid and captioned properly."

"Really?"

"Yes."

"I would appreciate the opportunity." Mr Simms bowed slightly, then straightened up. "Blast, the bus. Come on. Photography isn't going to feed my children, and I really need this job."

"Blame us. The driver wouldn't dare leave anyone behind." Reiko shrugged and it was yet another reminder of how she walked between different worlds so easily. She spoke to Mr Simms with the ease of being his equal, a colleague, which made sense given that she worked at a bar and understood the demands of his job, and yet she also assumed the bus would wait for her simply because of her family connections. Yolande wanted to wrap Reiko up and hold her tight. The idea sent a cold chill over the back of her neck; one kiss and she falling for Reiko. She missed Captain and Bounce, and just wanted to go home and cuddle them. Life with her cats was simple. Stepping into a relationship was anything but simple.

10

———

Reiko couldn't believe the quality of photos Mr Simms had created, using just her phone camera and clever use of light and angles. She wanted to frame the one of herself draped in Yolande's arms. The soft sunshine through the stained glass windows created shadows on Yolande's face, each one highlighting her beauty and somehow capturing the juxtaposition between her strength and vulnerability. Her brunette bob-cut conveyed motion, with one strand clinging to her temple, out of place, and the lack of perfection added to the drama and realness of the scene.

The bus drove along a typical narrow laneway from the church back to the main house, with the driver hitting the horn at every corner in an oddly gentle reminder that he was coming through. Reiko didn't rate their chances of getting past another vehicle if one came from the opposite direction.

"The photos are amazing." Yolande sounded subdued. Hopefully, she wasn't overthinking their kiss or worse, regretting it.

"Mr Simms is incredibly talented."

"You meant what you said back there?"

"I always do." The idea that Yolande would doubt her promise to Mr Simms shook her to her core and she couldn't help but glance askew at her. After a long silence, during which Reiko ran back over their important conversations, she conceded that her behaviour last night probably gave Yolande the impression that she'd fudge the truth to suit the occasion. It was what everyone did.

"Obviously there are times when I'm uncertain about what I want or have misconstrued a situation, but I always speak my truth and I keep my promises."

Yolande side-eyed her. "And that's supposed to reassure me?"

"Yes. A blanket statement guaranteeing complete truth isn't possible. Not for humans, who are flawed, and even when they aren't, people change their views when they acquire more information." Reiko's academic work high-lighted the complexity of people and habit meant she tried not to use either/or language to describe anything.

"That's too complicated for me. How did we end up in the discussion?"

"You asked if I would keep my promise to Mr Simms and show Father his photos. I wanted to be clear that I always keep my promises, and I tell the truth as I understand it at the time."

Yolande rolled her eyes. "Yeah, clear as fucking mud. Can you hear how slippery that makes you sound? Is this why you don't talk much when you are working at Seraph's?"

"What do you mean?" Reiko reeled from the change in Yolande. She stiffened up at the accusations, wanting to defend herself, even though some of it was warranted. She didn't talk because she liked to help and to listen. Besides, almost everyone at Seraph's knew more about burlesque than her.

"I've seen a side of you during this wedding that I didn't expect and I'm uncertain how it fits with the person I knew before. Where is the Reiko who charmed my cat?"

"Still here. I'm still the same." Except she knew exactly what Yolande meant. She wasn't the same here as she was at Seraph's, nor was she the same as she was with her PhD supervisor. She spent her life fitting into different places, never quite being her whole self anywhere.

"But you just said you live a different truth depending on the situation?"

Reiko tried not to cringe as Yolande made her sound like Father. Had she learned too many nasty habits from him? Were her efforts to tell the truth always and not be like him all for nothing? She breathed in slowly and held her breath as she recognised the extreme language of her thoughts. Various therapists and her academic training over the years meant she tried to avoid simplistic rigid thinking; reality was often more nuanced, less extreme, and finding a middle ground was the journey towards more helpful thoughts.

"I didn't say that. Perhaps I explained myself badly?"

Yolande cleared her throat. "People always say that when they want to cast doubt."

"Shit. I'm sorry." Reiko wanted to dive under the bus seat. This was why she didn't talk, because when she did, she made a mess of it. "You are right."

"About what?" Why couldn't Yolande let this go? Where had this all gone wrong?

"Everything?"

"Oh, now that's bollocks."

Reiko willed the bus to arrive at Rutheringholme, so she could hide somewhere, away from all people, especially Yolande. Except she was here to support her, and besides their room had only one bed. Fuck. What a tangle she'd twisted herself into, and she wasn't even sure exactly how she'd ended up here. She'd tried to explain how truth was marred by individual perspective, when it seemed like Yolande wanted more certainty than Reiko could provide. Was that it?

She kept her mouth shut and just stared at the back of the seat in front of her. Thankfully this bus was mostly empty and she wasn't forced into conversation with anyone except Yolande. Her friend, whom she'd just kissed. How much had she just messed everything up? Of course, it was all she deserved, because of her habit of keeping her emotions under a tight lid constantly, so that when they escaped, they created damage. Now who was being dramatic and extreme?

"Shit. Are you crying?" Yolande wiped her face and Reiko sniffed.

"No." She was only leaking a few emotions, nothing as serious as crying.

"I thought you always told the truth."

"Fine." Reiko couldn't keep in the tension anymore. The whole fiasco with her parents being here, meeting Anne again and discovering she was a Duchess, being on parade in society, and most of all, kissing Yolande. It was all too much. A loud sob caught in her throat, stuck there unable to escape. Fuck. Could she hold it together until they arrived back at Rutheringholme? Hopefully.

"You don't look fine." *Pity.* That's what rang in Yolande's voice and Reiko hated it. People shouldn't feel sorry for her. Look at her life; she had exactly what she wanted. A doctorate in an important subject that hadn't been explored yet. A good job helping people at Seraph's. And this… the life she had been trained to survive in. Blergh. Survive or thrive? There were many good reasons why she avoided parties like this one, and the biggest reason of all was that she hated the way she behaved, hated the person she was when surrounded by other rich people. Simply saying that inside her head sounded like a big winge. Well, she'd rather complain than cry. Wouldn't she? A salty tear slid into the corner of her mouth. It tasted like failure. Failure to conform, failure to stay away, failure to be herself, failure to tell her friends at Seraph's about her money. Having Yolande question who she was only added to the pain inside her.

Stop. Stop blaming Yolande for these feelings. Reiko had done this to herself; she'd wanted to show off to Yolande, to prove she was better for her than Helen, that she could give Yolande this world and this life, when Helen had ditched her to be part of it. Oh, now that was a tangled web.

"Come on. Let's get off the bus and go to our room." Yolande laid her hand gently over Reiko's hand and she let herself be led off the bus. Far too many people were standing outside Rutheringholme. The staff were handing out champagne, and most people were watching Brian and Helen get more photos taken on the lawn. It stretched away into the view, a perfect example of a Capability Brown landscape. There had to be a side entrance to the house, or a way she could avoid this crowd. Avoiding crowds was her speciality.

"Excuse me, Mr Simms?"

"Yes?"

"Is there a way we could skirt around these people and go up to our room without being noticed?" Reiko couldn't look at Yolande as she asked.

"Of course. Come with me." Mr Simms stepped between them and the crowd of people and ushered them around the corner of the building. Thankfully, the crowd was over on the front steps and lawn and the bus had parked away from the crowd. Most of those on the bus had already wandered over to join the crowd, so by following Mr Simms they could make their escape without being seen.

"Are you ill? Do you need anything?"

"No. Just a little overwhelmed."

"I understand. It's a big event."

Reiko could hear Yolande's footsteps half a stride behind her. No, she wouldn't freak out and ask her what she was thinking. It would do no one any good if she demanded to know why Yolande thought she was a terrible person. No good at all. Soon enough, Mr Simms opened a door and gave them quick directions to the main staircase. Reiko scampered up the stairs as fast as her gown would allow and rushed into their room with a huge sigh. She fell on the bed —with enough drama for the stage—and tried to stop the rampaging negative spiral of thoughts. Spiral. Oh. Her heart raced and she realised it had been doing that for a while now.

"I'm sorry. I need some space." Reiko glanced at Yolande, who stood by the window. What Reiko needed was to talk to her therapist. Having someone on call was a huge privilege but also necessary when something like this happened. These episodes—almost panic attacks—were less frequent than they used to be, in fact, she couldn't remember the last one. It must have been three years ago? The regular weekly sessions were working. Hope managed to filter through her panic as she closed the bathroom door behind her and dialled Taylor's number.

Yolande had never been so confused in her entire fucking life. In the space of less than an hour, she'd experienced the best kisses of her life, and then the whole thing in the church had made her feel so inadequate. But that didn't explain why Reiko had turned on her with an out-of-character rudeness, then cried. What the fuck was going on?

One thing was true, if kisses had this effect on Reiko, then neither of them were ready for a relationship. Was it out of character? Or did Reiko think those unsettling thoughts while she was Seraph's, quietly watching everyone? Yolande didn't even care anymore that Helen had left. All her focus was absorbed by wanting to fix Reiko. Oh. She was doing it again. If she was alone at this wedding, what would she do? Pour a big fucking drink because they were free, and then she'd make the most of this situation and enjoy herself.

She poured the drink. A faint whisper came through the bathroom door, followed by soft sobs, and she put the drink down. She couldn't drink and pretend to be enjoying life while Reiko was upset. Reiko, who was always there for everyone else. Reiko, with the judgemental father. Reiko, who juggled her life between this one that'd been forced on her, and the one she lived in London. At no point since they'd arrived had Reiko been snobbish to Yolande. If she thought back over everything, Reiko had gone out of her way to help Yolande feel comfortable, and as soon as she'd needed support of her own, Yolande had been too caught up in how she didn't belong here and felt inadequate to be able to help Reiko. Oh. What a shitty way to behave. Reiko's tears made sense and she needed to apologise. She poured another whisky, then eased the door open and passed the drink through the crack.

"Thank you. Sorry. Hold on a minute… Yolande. I'm sorry, I'll just be a little longer. Thank you for the drink."

Yolande nodded. "It's no problem."

She shut the door again, then did what anyone else would do in this situation. She grabbed her phone and her drink and sank down into one of the large chairs beside the window. The view from their window was out over the local farmland, green rolling hills, and a little village with brick houses. She savoured the warmth of the whisky as she swallowed, then looked at her phone. Shit, her notifications were out of control. The Seraph's chat group was the worst, with everyone making jokes about the wallpaper in the Peacock room. She chuckled as she read them, and then Reiko had added a couple of selfies from last night. Jeepers, they'd been bloody drunk when they'd taken these; she couldn't even remember taking them. It must have been after the cocktail party back in their room. The wallpaper gave away the location, but damn, they both had glassy eyes and looked messy. At least they were both still wearing their gowns in these photos; not that she cared. Everyone at Seraph's had seen her tits, hundreds of times. Reiko might not want that. Had Reiko seen the way Ace had fawned over her pink gown?

He'd called it a replica Valli, which was hilarious, a private joke that she wanted to share with Reiko.

Further down the thread, Reiko had uploaded a couple of photos from the church. Yes, she agreed with everyone else. Helen did look stunning in that gown, and the church was like something from a Disney movie.

The door opened, and Reiko walked out, drying her face on a towel.

"I'm not very good at admitting this, but you were right. I do find it… not impossible, but very difficult, to belong. I don't fit here because I can't be the person Father wants me to be. And I don't fit anywhere else, because as soon as people find out about all of this, then they look at me differently. I freaked out, and I'm sorry."

"It's okay. Thank you for explaining. You shouldn't be sorry for freaking out. Are you alright? I was worried about you." And Yolande needed to make an apology of her own. Her own version of freaking out had started this whole mess.

"I will be alright in a while. I've just had a good chat to Taylor, my therapist, and she reminded me that I'm not responsible for the way Father talks to me. I'm working on unlearning some of my behaviours, and I'm sorry you had to see me acting like that."

Yolande paused. "Don't be sorry. I really like you, Reiko. All of you. The quiet helper at Seraph's that no one notices, the cat charmer, the person who texted me every day when Helen devastated me. And the person you are in this society. I like that part of you too."

"But you said I wasn't being honest with you?"

"No. You said that. I was merely confused about why your comment about truth came with such a disclaimer."

"It didn't." Reiko glared, then slowly shook her head. "It did. Why can't I stop being like that?"

"Do you want to stop?"

"Yes. Because it makes me into an asshole." The vehemence in Reiko's voice nearly knocked Yolande off her chair, something of a feat given the way it cradled her.

"Listen to yourself, Reiko. You couldn't be an asshole if you tried. Last night, you had every opportunity to make Helen pay for how she treated me, and what did you do? You requested … no, you *insisted* that she apologise to me, then you introduced her to a fucking Duchess. You gave her what she craved. How does that make you an asshole?"

"I don't know."

"Just because people are assholes to you, doesn't mean that you are the same in return. Sometimes when you need to fight for something, you don't realise that you fight for everything. You can just be."

"Just be?"

"Yes. Embrace your imperfect, messy self." Yolande tried not to cringe at her own advice. She'd never been as good at taking advice as she was at giving it out. "Speaking of which, I have an apology of my own."

"Whatever for?"

"The whole argument on the bus was my fault."

"No." Reiko shook her head.

Yolande stood up and gently took the towel from Reiko's hands. "It was. Being in the church, listening to you laugh with Mr Simms about rich people liking their photos taken made me feel inadequate." She held up her palm. "Wait. Please. I love getting my photo taken. I love it when people take photos of my shows and put them on social media. But

I'm not rich, and in that moment I knew I'd never belong in this world with you. So I started an argument as a defensive tactic, and I'm sorry."

"Oh." Reiko closed her eyes for a long moment. When she opened them, they were filled with compassion. "If it makes you feel better, I never feel like I belong in this world either."

"Aren't we a pair?" Yolande wished she could erase the whole argument on the bus and the way it had upset Reiko so deeply. "A lot has happened since we arrived here. I feel like I'm going to need a few weeks just to let it all settle down."

Reiko's phone vibrated in her hand. She glanced at it, frowned, then threw it on the bed. "Sorry. Mum wants to go for a walk in the gardens this afternoon before the big wedding dinner tonight."

"Do you want to go?"

"Yes. I miss her. But I also want to hide in here for a while."

Yolande grinned. "How about we hide here together for a while, then go for that walk with your mother together?"

"You want to come with us?"

"I want to support you. You've been a really good friend to me, especially since Helen left, and if you need me to come along, then I will. Otherwise, just do whatever you need."

"Okay. But first, I want to know what you mean when you say a lot has happened since we arrived here."

Yolande gulped. It was funny how she hadn't realised she'd wanted Reiko to ignore that comment and move on, but she also really wanted to talk about it all and have someone listen. "Are you ready for this?"

"Sure."

"Right. Remember on the drive up here, we talked about sharing the cost of the trip; you'd get the food and I'd get the fuel?" At Reiko's nod, Yolande shook her head and grinned. "The food was always going to cost less than the fuel and I was cool with that because you are a student who works in a bar, so I assumed you wouldn't have much money and I have a good full time job, so I was happy with spending more on the fuel."

"Do you want some money for fuel?"

"No. I really don't. You came to support me as I watch my ex get married, honestly that's worth more than money."

"Okay…"

"My point was that I made assumptions about you, then we got here, and you were so comfortable with the whole place. All my assumptions were wrong, and it's been a lot to process."

Reiko frowned. "That's why I don't tell people. Everyone sees the money and treats me differently."

"Have I done that? I really hope I haven't."

"No, you've been fine. I just don't see what the big deal is, or why it needs thinking about."

Yolande almost joked about how only someone who had everything could call it not a big deal, but she stopped herself. Now wasn't the time for jokes or potential misunderstandings. "It's not a big deal. I was surprised, that's all. And this whole place has been a bit overwhelming as an experience. There are all these rules and people who know each other, and I don't belong and…"

"I know exactly what you mean."

"You do?"

"Yolande. How many times have we talked about me not belonging anywhere? It's worse than that. The real problem is that I do belong here. I just don't want to."

Yolande nodded. "That makes a lot of sense. I only mentioned it because it was a big shift in my assumptions. I thought we'd be in the same boat when we turned up, both out of our depth arriving as a student and a nurse to this fucking fancy house to watch Helen getting married to a bloody Earl's son. Like, that alone is a weird mind-fuck anyway."

Reiko gave her such a compassionate look, Yolande couldn't understand how Reiko could imagine she was anything but caring. "Did you want to talk about that?"

"About?"

"Watching Helen get married."

"It's weird, right? I came here to prove to myself that I could still be her friend and support her, even when her choices hurt me. But what I've realised is that I don't have to do that. She hurt me. She chose this world, and she probably doesn't know how kind you were last night when you introduced her to the Duchess."

"Kind?" Reiko scoffed. "Anne is going to tear her to shreds if she's not careful."

"I don't understand."

Reiko shrugged. "Anne and Helen have a lot in common —they are grifters in a man's world—except Helen doesn't have Anne's experience amongst this class. Anne was born into wealth and she's made choices that have taken her advantages and made the most of them. Helen has no advantages apart from great tits, so she's disadvantaged because she doesn't know the rules and Anne will chew her up and spit her out if she's not careful… Anyway, none of that crap matters. It's none of our business how they chose to live their life." For someone who barely spoke at work, Reiko was a lot chattier when it was just the two of them.

"That all makes sense. Good luck to her. I was so gutted when she left…" Yolande swallowed the bitter taste hovering on her tongue. "With time, and seeing her here, all that I feel is, I don't know, a little bit of pettiness whenever she looks overwhelmed, but mostly just sadness. I'm sad for her because she's never going to be happy as she continues to chase the next thing, and I'm sad for me. I gave up so much of myself for her and she just—"

"Threw you away?"

Yolande choked on a gasp. "Yes. How do you make those callous words sound so caring?"

11

"Excuse me?" But Reiko knew what Yolande meant. She'd deliberately used that phrase because she couldn't understand why the hell Helen had left Yolande in a way that was so … callous. Just like Yolande said.

"Somehow your tone implies that you care for me."

Reiko blinked. "Why does that confuse you? We've just spent half the morning kissing."

"Of course." Something in Yolande's tone stung, as if their kisses didn't matter that much. Those moments spent kissing had been everything for Reiko, the moment of connection she wanted for years. All that pining and yearning released as she finally, finally, kissed Yolande. To know that it wasn't the same for Yolande stung like a thousand bees and she wanted to swat it all away. Agreeing to be Yolande's plus one for this wedding had been a bad idea from the very beginning and now all her concerns were coming to fruition. When this weekend was over, her already bruised heart was going to hurt for a long time. She shouldn't have taken the risk because her feelings were already one-sided and unrequited before they'd arrived here. Now they'd kissed and Reiko would forever know what she was missing out on.

"That's what I've been trying to say. This whole weekend has been a mind fuck. I could never have imagined wanting to kiss you until recently."

"Ouch." Reiko feigned ambivalence as her heart shattered into tiny pieces.

"Oh fuck. I'm sorry. I didn't mean that." Bright red spots appeared on Yolande's cheeks, and Reiko wanted to ask her what she did mean. Nothing came out, just short heavy breaths.

"How could I have been so oblivious? It's taken me this disaster of a wedding to realise how little attention I have paid to you. I think we all have. Everyone at Seraph's just takes you for granted—" Gee, Yolande was really rubbing it in now. Reiko stood tense and taut, trying not to crumble. Her breath stung in her lungs and every muscle shook with lactic acid from standing so stiffly.

"And we shouldn't have done that. You are amazing. A wonderful friend."

Reiko growled under her breath. "And rich." It was so bloody predictable for Yolande to finally see her as a person, as a friend, after she'd met her parents and seen her wearing a fucking two thousand pound designer dress. This always happened; it was why she didn't tell anyone. Coming here had been a risk, but she'd assumed—wrongly—that a third son marrying a nobody wouldn't be like this, and certainly wouldn't necessitate her parents flying in from Japan for such an event. She breathed out slowly; they'd come for her, not the wedding, and wasn't she a terrible daughter for not inviting them to spend time with her before now? Taylor's gentle voice managed to sneak past the start of a negative spiral of voices. *Boundaries matter.* She wasn't a terrible daughter for having boundaries. It was okay if it was complicated.

"No, I was going to say, fucking sexy and the best kisser ever."

"What?" Reiko must have heard her wrong. *Say it again.* Just so she could be sure of it. She dared not let out her breath and hope.

"I changed myself for Helen and she didn't respect me. What I've come to realise is that the person I need to be is me, and then I'll be appreciated by someone who sees the real me." Yolande laughed softly under her breath, the sound irritating Reiko's skin, like a fork scratching on a ceramic plate. "The irony of it all is that you've been there the whole time. I'm the one who has missed out, so caught up in trying to be what Helen wanted me to be, that I missed the most important thing."

Did she dare ask what that might be? No. She just waited.

"You. Of course it's you, Reiko."

"Are you certain it's not the money?"

Yolande frowned. "What?"

"This always happens. People don't notice me until they learn who my parents are, then suddenly I'm thrust into this role as being important to them. 'I can't believe I overlooked you until now.'" She mocked the phrase she'd heard multiple times in her life. It reinforced that she was nothing without her trust fund.

"Okay. The timing sucks. Trust me, it's not about the

money. I've met your father and his disrespect for you only showed me how tough you are. You care for the people around you, and that matters more to me than the money. Finding out about the money was a shock, that's all."

"That's what everyone says. Oh, you are rich, suddenly we notice how kind you are to everyone, and how much we want to be your friend." She'd been hurt so often by people who did this that she couldn't trust Yolande to be any different. Evidence be damned.

"I've always been your friend, Reiko. Sometimes I've been a bad friend, caught up in the impossible, trying to please Helen, but that hasn't changed between us."

"So it is just the money that has changed things then?" Reiko was bored with this conversation. She'd done this ad infinitum during her life, and it was extra disappointing to hear the same old crap from Yolande. If she'd thought this through and hadn't been riding on futile hopes, she should've seen this coming. The tension disappeared from her limbs because it didn't matter anymore. Wherever she went, no one really saw her, and she helped them all by bending to the situation.

"No. Like I said, the timing sucks. I asked you to come here with me, because I knew I would need a good friend at my side. It was foolish of me to come here. I thought that watching Helen get married would give me closure. It would make it final; there was no chance for a reconciliation. But I don't feel that at all."

"You still want Helen?"

"No. Not in the slightest. I guess I did get closure from that point of view." Yolande rolled her head on her shoulders and stretched her arms. Watching her casually move her dancer's body usually gave Reiko a thrill. Not now. "Being here showed me the truth."

"And that is?" There was zero chance of lust while Reiko had to deal with another friend—and this one a potential lover and brilliant kisser—raved on about how it wasn't the money when they both knew it was the money. Boring aspirational nonsense, and the same old excuses she'd heard a million times about how someone truly noticed her now. Blergh.

"From the day she left, you were there. You helped me get through that godawful dance that night and I didn't feel so alone knowing that my kitty was there, nodding encouragingly, so I could keep going while my heart was breaking. You helped me look for my lucky crystal. You listened when I said I couldn't stay afterwards that night, and you put me in a rideshare so I would get home safely while too emotional to cope with public transport and all that. And you sent me a text every day afterwards to make sure I was okay. You cared. That's the truth."

Reiko didn't want to believe Yolande, but her heart thudded happily regardless. All the times that other people had noticed her felt different to this. Maybe it was just because she'd been in love with Yolande forever, so it was easier for her to push aside her concerns and chase after what she wanted? Or maybe it was because Yolande truly was her friend. She hadn't mocked her when Reiko had told her she couldn't drive. Yolande had been genuinely upset when Father had been his usual self. The years of yearning cumulated in Reiko needing to be with Yolande more than she cared about being certain it wasn't the money. If it was the money, she'd find out in time. Until then, she could have kisses.

"Okay." She walked towards Yolande, and with each step she pushed away her own worries. She was going to kiss Yolande, take a chance, and be with her. She'd waited too long.

"Even my cats adore you. Is it any wonder I want to be with you?"

"You do?"

"I shouldn't. Not so soon after being discarded by Helen, but I do. I really do."

Reiko stretched up to wrap her arms around Yolande's shoulders. She had to stand on tiptoes to reach. Really, she shouldn't have kicked off her heels. Heels would make this kiss closer, easier, and yet it didn't matter, as Yolande bent her head and soft wet lips touched hers. If anything could make Reiko believe in the two of them, it was this kiss. Sensation ruled, a rush of sensation flooding her veins with heat and need, as they kissed. Reiko stepped so her legs were either side of Yolande's long thigh, and she ground herself against the lean muscle.

The kiss was an indulgence, a glorious joining that stole away all her thoughts and only the rhythm of their kiss mattered. Yolande fumbled with Reiko's zip, then slowly—too slowly—eased the zipper down her side.

"Off."

"Huh?" Reiko jumped backwards at the command. Did Yolande want to get off her body? But no, Yolande stroked the frown between Reiko's eyebrows, soothing it even though Reiko hadn't realised she was frowning.

"I want to take your dress off. One kiss, and all I want to do is strip you naked and kiss you everywhere."

Reiko nodded. A flutter of self-consciousness tried to flare up and stop her, but she shook it off. For years, she'd wanted this, and she wasn't going to let a little lack of confidence stop her. Yolande was a dancer; fit and strong and flexible; while Reiko was… Well, fit enough from her work at the bar, but nothing special.

"Can I?"

"Yes. Please." Reiko brushed her dress off her own shoulders, letting the gorgeous yellow fabric float down her body to the ground. She stepped out of it, careful not to tramp on it and rip the fabric, then she bent down to pick up the dress. As she shook it out, and laid it across a chair, Yolande laughed.

"Once a kitty, always a kitty."

Reiko hummed a vague answer. The hum turned into a moan as Yolande stroked her fingers up the back of Reiko's thighs, with just enough fingernail scratch to make the sensation sharp.

"You like that?"

"Yes." Her voice had gone all raspy. Yolande stroked her thighs again, this time with one hand placed in the middle of Reiko's back.

"Stay like that." Yolande's command came from nowhere. Reiko wouldn't have picked Yolande as someone who liked to give orders in bed, but damn, she loved it. She'd always found it hard to ask for what she wanted; half the time when she went out, people would flirt with her and it wouldn't be until afterwards that she'd realise what they'd wanted. Maybe she needed someone to guide her. Yolande was doing a spectacular job, with one hand holding her in place, bent over the chair, and the other sliding up one thigh, across the top of her bottom, then down the other side. On repeat. A slow arch that transferred sensation from one leg to the other, while building pressure in Reiko's pussy. She moaned, needing more. Needing to turn around and touch Yolande herself.

"If I took these off, what would you do?" Yolande plucked her panties. *Fall in a puddle of desire?* Reiko's breath was so short and fast that she couldn't answer. She tried, and only a groan came out. Her knees wobbled and she clutched the chair tighter.

"You like that idea, don't you?"

"Yes."

"I have a better one."

"Oh?" Reiko panted as Yolande's fingers skirted the edge of her panties, so close, but not close enough. Yolande slid her hands up so she held Reiko's waist, then higher along her spine, until she rested them on her shoulders. Her body leaned over Reiko's, barely touching her, heat radiating over her skin. Yolande kissed the back of her neck.

"Come with me."

Reiko's pussy clenched a little at the command. It wouldn't take much for her to actually come. "Where?"

Yolande stood up, taking all her heat with her. She trailed her fingertips down Reiko's spine again, sending shivers scattered across her skin. "With me." Yolande tapped her hand gently on Reiko's arse and she jerked in response.

"Do you like that?"

"Maybe? It was unexpected, that's all." Reiko had never experienced anything like it, and she couldn't decide if she wanted more, or if she was just accepting it because it was Yolande.

"I'm sorry. I should have asked." Yolande tugged on her shoulders. "Here, stand up."

Reiko stood up and slowly turned around to face Yolande. Her cheeks burned with heat and Yolande's soft expression did nothing to stop the glow.

"I'm probably overthinking it."

Yolande frowned. "No. I'm the one who overstepped. I'm sorry. Can I kiss you now?"

"Yes please." Reiko had read enough romance novels to know that people liked all sorts of things that she wasn't sure she'd be comfortable with. The slight tap had been exhilarating. She'd gasped, but why? From pleasure or shock? All thoughts disappeared as Yolande bent her head and kissed her. Kisses, she could understand. She definitely wanted to kiss Yolande. The kiss was familiar now, still thrilling, with that unbelievable taste of Yolande. After so long wanting and watching and not receiving, this kiss was like the final anticipation had been completed and satisfied.

"I think I have too many clothes on." Yolande stepped backwards and stripped off her dress. The fabric made a puddle of navy on the floor. Sunlight streamed in the large windows of the Peacock room, giving Yolande a wholesome healthy glow on her olive skin and brunette locks. She wore matching navy blue bra and undies—of course—with lace cupping the edges of her breasts. Reiko swallowed, unable to speak with such beauty taking up the whole view.

"Come on." Yolande beckoned, the gesture familiar from her time on stage, and Reiko shook her head.

"No, don't dance for me. I don't want a performance."

She wanted the real version, the truth behind the burlesque façade.

"Then you'll have to undress me."

"What?"

"Burlesque is about power. When I dance, I have all the power. I choose what to remove and when. If you want something different, then you need to take that from me."

Reiko frowned and ignored the way her fingers twitched with wanting. "No. I don't want either of us to take. That's not a language that works for me."

"Oh?"

"Sex…" Reiko cleared her throat. "Sex is about pleasure. About giving. That's what I want."

Yolande smiled, a huge slashing smile that made her whole face glow. "You are a gift. It seems I have some habits to unlearn."

"Later." Reiko had waited too long for all this talking. She jogged across the room and pulled Yolande into a hug. It was easy to stand on tiptoes and kiss her again, and even easier to spread her hands over Yolande's skin. Skin that she'd seen hundreds of times before, but never touched. Now she was touching her soft skin, and it was everything. A mess of sensations that built as pressure in her core until she was humming into Yolande's mouth. Yolande's perfume, a heady mix of florals and mint, surrounded her, like summer days and long sunny afternoons. Reiko flicked at Yolande's bra, opening up the hooks and releasing her breasts. She cupped them, cherishing their weight. The long wait had been worthwhile. Yolande's firm dancer's muscles were long and lean under Reiko's hands as she stroked and explored all of Yolande's spectacular body. Each movement came naturally, as if her body knew exactly what it wanted. Together they walked, lips locked, to the bed, and soon they tumbled together onto the huge mattress. A giggle escaped. One quickly hidden in another kiss. Soon, Yolande was kissing down Reiko's neck, and lower, with her bare breasts gliding over Reiko's small tits and stomach, until she nestled between Reiko's legs.

"Why are you still dressed?"

"Why are you?" Reiko teased, amazed that she could talk as Yolande's bob-cut tickled her bare stomach. Gooseflesh chased the motion of Yolande's hair, and it wasn't until Yolande brushed her belly a few more times, that Reiko realised she did it on purpose. Laughter spilled out and she reached for Yolande's scalp, gently pushing her head lower.

"You want me to lick you?"

Reiko couldn't breathe. "Mmmm, yeah." She managed something like consent.

"Are you sure? I want to taste you, to lick you, and fill you with my tongue. But you have to say yes."

Oh dear. What delicious torture. "Yes, please. Yolande." Reiko's consent sounded breathy with a little rasp as if she'd screamed her yes until she'd injured her voice.

"As you wish." Yolande shifted a little more, pushing Reiko's thighs apart, and settling between. Her fingers drifted all over Reiko's skin, sliding under her panties, then not. Teasing and taunting in the very best way. When Yolande tugged her panties down, Reiko used her hands to help, somehow ending up breathless as she tried to slide them down her legs. Her legs and Yolande's body were all tangled and she had to pull one leg up to her chest, and slide her panties off that leg only. Yolande's hum of appreciation as Reiko stretched and exposed herself was golden. Her breath on Reiko's slick clit was even better and Reiko shuddered as her body burned with need.

"Please." Reiko's rasp worsened, then descended into a strangled groan when Yolande covered her with her mouth. The wet heat of her mouth over her pussy was a more glorious sensation than Reiko could deal with; the surging desire in her veins threatened to boil over. She threaded her hands into Yolande's hair and clung onto it as Yolande licked and sipped and sucked. Each touch of her tongue on Reiko's clit made her moan and her hips bucked. Reiko's fingers tightened on Yolande's head, pulling her hair with a need that came from deep inside her. When Yolande spread her wide with her fingers, and thrust her tongue inside, Reiko screamed.

"Wait." Yolande's soft command halted Reiko mid-pant, and she couldn't breathe. Yolande pressed her fingers on Reiko's clit and she couldn't wait anymore. She gasped for breath, arching her body, wanting more.

"I can't wait."

Yolande slid her fingers inside Reiko, then sucked her clit hard, once. She lifted her head for half a second. "Go." A cool blast of Yolande's breath over her clit sent shards of heat spiralling through her torso, and when Yolande nipped at her again, Reiko let go. She came with a rush of warm heat, pushing herself hard against Yolande's face. Hungry noises and gulps of air filled the room, and Reiko's body trembled and shook as her orgasm took charge. The pleasure was intense, pulsing passionately until she was wrung out. Her eyes were all heavy and her limbs relaxed until she was barely aware of Yolande crawling up her body to kiss her. Her own musk scented Yolande's tongue, and a fresh shiver ran along her spine.

"Look at you all hazy and flushed. So beautiful." Yolande brushed Reiko's hair out of her face. The tender touch dragged her back to the real world.

"What about you?" Her whisper was barely audible but Yolande smiled as if she'd heard.

"Oh, I'm fine."

"But you didn't come?"

"Not yet, no." Yolande rubbed her pubic bone against Reiko's thigh, and Reiko gasped again.

"Let me." Reiko had wanted to do one thing for years. This was her chance, so she forced her sated muscles to move. She rolled them both over, until Yolande was under her on the bed. With lazy circles, she traced Yolande's body. Along her ribs, under her tits, along her collarbone, over her strong defined stomach muscles. Almost down to her panties. Not this time, but the next time she went past and cupped her. Her lingerie was soaked. Perfect.

Reiko pressed a kiss to Yolande's mouth, then dragged her lips down Yolande's neck, one hand lightly on Yolande's lingerie, the other tangled in her hair. Each kiss and stroke of her lips against Yolande's skin tasted like home and fucking great sex. She'd never had sex like this before, where all she wanted to do was worship Yolande's gorgeous body. Reiko thanked her foresight in taking off Yolande's bra earlier and it made it easier to keep her hands spread in place while she licked her tits. Yolande wrapped her hands around Reiko's back, and her strong fingers tried to guide Reiko. She giggled breathily against Yolande's breast, waiting for a half-second before she sucked her nipple. Hard. The groan that

Yolande emitted was almost a scream. Not quite enough, so Reiko did it again, and this time, she curled her fingers where she cupped Yolande's sex. The scream was exactly right.

"More?"

"Please. Reiko. Where have you been?"

"Here. I've always been here." The truth didn't ache like usual. How could it, when Yolande clutched at her so wantonly?

Yolande hooked her long legs around Reiko's back, pulling her closer with such desperate need that Reiko wanted to keep giving her pleasure. She sucked and licked, and enjoyed every moan and scream, until Yolande began to beg. The breathy words of need filled Reiko's core with more heat, her own lungs panting for air. She slipped her hand inside Yolande's lingerie and between her folds, along her slick pussy, seeking out that little nugget of pleasure. Her clit. One flick by her thumb, then another, and another, each one punctuated with a matching kiss on Yolande's nipples, until Yolande screamed and writhed under her. She clenched around Reiko's fingers, and Reiko's own sex echoed the sensation with an orgasm of her own. Her body shuddered, absorbing Yolande's pleasure with her own, until she was breathless from the thrill of it.

They lay there for fuck knows how long with Reiko's head resting on Yolande's stomach.

"Shall we pretend we are too sick to attend the dinner tonight?" Yolande's suggestion was a king's ransom, one she wanted to take and screw the cost.

"I wish I could." Reiko didn't want to leave this bed. Technically, she didn't want to leave Yolande's side, happy to lie here with their limbs all tangled and bodies worn out by sex.

"Why can't you? This is Helen's wedding. We've done what we set out to achieve already. Let's stay in bed and play."

Reiko laughed. "Yeah, fuck my obligation to go for a walk with my Mum and then have dinner with my parents."

"Yeah, fuck them." Yolande giggled. "No. I'm sorry. We really have to go, don't we?"

"We do." Reiko sighed.

"But just think of the reward we'll both get afterwards." Yolande half-sat up, and the movement caused Reiko to roll slightly down her stomach. She dragged herself up into a seated position. Damn, her body felt so heavy and rested.

"I guess we'd better get ready." The real world beckoned, and there was one thing she probably should mention. "Can we avoid talking about where we met?"

"Why?"

"I'm proud of my work at Seraph's. I like helping, but my Mum would see it as demeaning and I would like to avoid a lecture on how it makes me look like a model minority." The stereotype existed but in Reiko's mind, it had nothing to do with the reasons why she loved her job at Seraph's.

"There's nothing demeaning about your job."

"I know that. I just want to avoid having the argument with my parents."

Yolande kissed her on the forehead. "Now that's a distinction I can understand. Come and have a shower and let me wash you."

"Oh." The idea expanded Reiko's imagination and she grinned. "I would like that very much."

"You couldn't possibly have dinner with your parents unless you are very clean. Inside and out." Yolande's smile was glorious, a reflection of the glow Reiko could feel on her own skin.

12

―――――

One thing became apparent to Yolande during the wedding dinner. It was going to take a lot of work to convince Reiko she wanted her for herself and not her money or connections. Yolande wanted Reiko for more than just incredible sex in the shower, although that was spectacular and had left her with a dreamy happiness that carried her through most of the dinner. The steamy heat of the water had added a mystical atmosphere allowing Yolande to get a little carried away in the moment. They'd covered each other in soap, laughing at the bubbles, and playing as they helped each other orgasm again and again.

Eventually, Yolande's fingers had gone all pruney and Reiko suggested they should turn the water off. and Yolande had reluctantly agreed, unwilling to move forward from their time together alone. They'd spent so long in the shower that Reiko had ended up calling her mother and apologising for missing their walk together.

It was great to see Reiko claim some space around her overbearing, judgemental, parents. Reiko was so responsive and kind, lavishing attention on Yolande, with kisses and lust and desire all wrapped up in a petite, fucking gorgeous, package. It was a tragedy that she'd been Reiko's friend for so long and been so oblivious to what was right here under her nose. Reiko's beauty was the type that was subtle and gentle and took time to appreciate. She'd taken her for granted for so long and now this incredible overwhelming desire to never let Reiko go had happened faster than she was able to process it. It was like her body knew what she wanted, and her brain had yet to catch up.

Throughout the dinner, Reiko had slowly lost her post-coital glazed stare and it was a terrible shame, as she was so beautiful in the throes of pleasure with her head thrown back and moans pouring out of her mouth. So wanton and a lovely private contrast to the buttoned-up version Reiko presented to the world. It was odd to think she'd seen Reiko in many guises; kitty, bar-helper, wealthy socialite, and sex goddess. And yet, Yolande wasn't sure she really knew Reiko completely. She had a gift for subtly transforming herself for each situation. Yolande sipped her wine, a gorgeous French Merlot with a sharp cherry base and the softest finish on her tongue. Rather like Reiko, who was complex and gentle, yet always herself in every situation; quiet, observant, unnoticed. Beautiful. If Yolande was brave enough to take a chance on a new relationship so soon after the disaster of what happened with Helen, she could become a true partner with Reiko. Was it too soon to be falling in love again?

"Yolande, how is the wine?" Reiko asked.

"Excellent." She cleared the roughness from her throat. "Thank you." *Thank you for coming here with me. Thank you for being so incredible.* Yolande had barely spoken throughout the dinner. There was too much to think about with regards to Reiko and she was so glad she wasn't sitting here alone at a table of strangers watching Helen get married. Helen, who had walked into the room wearing Yolande's lucky crystal—her blue lace agate—on a long necklace. Seeing it there, hanging between Helen's tits had taunted her through the whole dinner, until Yolande could barely speak for the rage rolling in her stomach. There were so many competing emotions for Yolande to process, which oddly made it easy to ignore them all and just focus on savouring the array of food on offer.

They'd started with an asparagus and truffle soup with yeasty fresh bread straight from the oven and herbed butter made on the Rutheringholme estate. For the next course, they'd had an artfully displayed spring salad with smoked trout, sourced from the nearby lake, with an indulgent sprinkle of caviar that made the whole dish pop. There was a palate cleanser between these, a vegetarian stack with aubergine, haloumi, zucchini, and fresh tomatoes, all drizzled with a caramelised balsamic reduction that added some tart and some sweet to the plate. By the time Yolande had been served the fourth course, she was tipsy on the matching wines, and of course, the wholesome local flavours of roast beef with Yorkshire puddings, perfect gravy, and creamed spinach, all seemed designed to send her into the blissful warmth of a food coma. Except for one thing.

Every other person in the room had drifted past their table during the evening and spoken to Reiko's Father at length about all sorts of stuff, reinforcing all the reasons why Reiko had been worried about the timing of Yolande paying her attention as well. The emotional shift during dinner had been gradual, with annoyance sneaking up on her until her stomach churned and her ears roared. If it wasn't for the little cheeky glances Reiko gave her all evening, Yolande was sure she would've exploded in anger.

The beef had been matched with a French merlot—the one she was sipping right now—and the generous serving size of the wine was at odds with the dainty size of the food. Each plate itself wasn't big, however, with so many different courses, it added up, just like the way people treated Reiko. Each interaction was nothing much when taken by itself. Over the dinner, they all added up, until Yolande understood Reiko's need to be seen for herself and not her connections. There was a deep frustration growing inside her that all these people only saw Reiko as a cypher for her parents, a person who was pleasant to chat to, as a stepping stone towards the connection they truly desired; aka Mr and Mrs Inoue, who were the real source of wealth.

If there was one thing Yolande knew to be true, it was how awful it was to be treated as a rung on a ladder, easily dismissed once someone climbed past. She'd been that person, that step, for Helen. The more she saw people doing the same thing, literally in action, around Reiko, the more it built like a simmering pressure cooker with no release valve.

Because it wasn't just the way others treated Reiko that had Yolande's emotions bubbling and foaming inside her. The assumption—one she'd made—that she had forgiven Helen and had moved on was wrong. So completely fucking wrong. The wedding this morning had made her nauseous, but she'd recovered valiantly, thanks in part to finally having sex with Reiko. However, it had been a temporary plaster on her emotions. Not that Reiko was a bandage to heal her wounds. Ergh. What a mess her head was.

Having to sit here and pretend to be polite while watching the sheer disrespect of so many of the guests who treated Reiko and her mother as ornaments, or worse, as softer targets in their aim to get an audience with Mr Inoue, combined with the fucking audacity of Helen wearing a stolen crystal to her wedding dinner until Yolande wanted to clutch her throat and let out a gigantic scream that would echo off the ridiculously high ceiling in the four-hundred-year-old ballroom. Phew. Holy fuck.

"What's the matter?" Reiko stood behind her chair with one hand on her shoulder and whispered.

"A lot."

"Oh?"

"Not here."

"Okay. Let me know if there is anything I can do."

Yolande tried not to growl. She wanted her crystal back. She wanted Reiko's father to truly notice how brilliant his daughter was, how she defied expectations by being herself with such quiet confidence. She wanted everyone else in the room to notice Reiko for herself. She wanted to drag Reiko back to bed like some sort of possessive monster and keep her there. The strength with which she wanted to cling to Reiko scared her deeply, causing a cold shiver across the back of her neck.

"Later." Damn, she wished she could pull that ugly tone back and replace it with something kinder. "It's not you." She glared in Helen's direction at her lucky crystal.

"Okay." Reiko squeezed her shoulder and wandered off, leaving Yolande to stew alone in her seat.

"Miss Cantor, how long have you been seeing my daughter?" Reiko's mother asked.

Yolande breathed in deep, unsure how to answer this question, when the reality was their first kiss had been this weekend. "We've been friends for a long time."

"That doesn't exactly answer my question."

"No, it doesn't."

"Maybe it's not our business." Mr Inoue surprised her, until it sunk in that it was more likely he didn't want to discuss his daughter's queer love life at a dinner like this. They were seated at a table of ten, five on each side, with Reiko's parents seated opposite her and Reiko. The six people at the other end of the table had chatted about nothing consequential for most of the dinner so far.

"Reiko was surprised to see you here at this wedding." Yolande changed the subject.

"Yes, it couldn't be helped. I didn't want to tell her we were coming and then have to cancel if the trip didn't work out. I didn't want to disappoint her." Mrs Inoue made a perfectly reasonable point.

"That makes sense. Even with the vaccine rollout, travel has still been tricky. I'm sure Reiko is glad you could make it here."

"You are sure? You don't know?" Mrs Inoue raised one eyebrow.

Yolande sipped her wine again. "I have discussed this with Reiko. It's not my place to discuss her opinion on matters without having asked her first." She'd already overstepped the bounds of consent once and in a way that was easily forgiven with an apology. She wouldn't do it again.

"I like the way you say that. You care for my daughter,

yes?"

"Yes. Very much." Finally, one question she didn't need to think about before answering.

"How did you meet? Was it at the hospital during the pandemic?" Mr Inoue considered her with an unsubtle look.

"Why do you ask that?" Yolande needed some time, unsure if Reiko's parents knew she worked at Seraph's. Not everyone was open minded about the existence of Seraph's Burlesque Club. Yolande knew all too well how people judged burlesque dancers in the same ugly way they judged strippers and sex workers. People like that could fuck right off—sex work was real work—but now wasn't exactly the time to have the argument about why people judged those doing the work, and not those paying for it.

"Who is asking what?" Reiko came to the rescue just as Yolande was floundering.

"Your father wants to know how we met. He guessed that we might have met at my work." For someone who'd only just stated that it was none of his business, he was quite interested in them.

"The hospital? Father, why?"

"Forgive me for having a small imagination—" Father's comment made Reiko cough quietly as she slipped back into her seat beside Yolande.

"No one would dare suggest such a thing," Reiko whispered.

"I heard that. Stop prevaricating, daughter. How else would you meet a nurse but at a hospital, and why didn't you tell us you were sick? We would have ensured you got the best of care."

Reiko patted Yolande on the knee, which was good

because the implication that her hospital—one of the best public hospitals in London—wasn't enough for the daughter of some rich guy made the noise in her ears grow in decibels.

"I wasn't sick. We met before the pandemic, at a bar, like many people do."

"Why haven't we heard of Miss Cantor before now?"

"Father, you made it perfectly clear that you had no interest in my lifestyle." Reiko kept her chin high as she spoke. It was unlikely that anyone heard the slight tremble in Reiko's voice; except Yolande had been paying close attention to Reiko lately and she noticed. She laid her hand over Reiko's and rubbed her thumb over her wrist.

"I've changed my mind."

"And was I ever going to be informed of this change? Or were you going to let me continue to think you didn't want to know, then proceed to feel aggrieved when I did something without your permission."

Mr Inoue frowned. "You are a grown woman. You don't need my permission to do anything; you haven't for some time."

"So why the sudden interest?" Colour washed over Reiko's cheeks.

"Perhaps this topic is a little indelicate to be having right now." Mr Inoue backed off. One of the people at the other end of the table shuffled in their seat and Yolande tried not to laugh at the way they were so obviously eavesdropping on the whole conversation. It was a huge relief to have something to focus on that wasn't her lucky crystal. She'd been on the brink of marching up to the bride's table and snatching it off Helen's neck; something that wouldn't endear her to anyone.

"Are you suggesting that my relationship is indelicate? How old fashioned of you." Reiko didn't raise her voice, something Yolande only noticed because she wanted to stomp her feet and yell.

"Not in the slightest. I'm only concerned about your… friend's motivation in being with you."

Reiko chuckled. Surely, everyone heard the undercurrent of sarcasm in her laugh. "Father, relax. Yolande didn't know about—" Reiko waved her hand around the room, ending her wave with a casual finger point in her father's direction. "—until this weekend. I'm not foolish, Father. I've lived my whole life with people only seeing you and not me."

Mr Inoue preened a little at that. "Clever. And does your Miss Cantor pass your test?"

"So far, although some aspects of this weekend have been challenging. I've been rightly accused of not being honest about myself, but it's amazing how an open discussion can illuminate someone's understanding."

Yolande grinned and squeezed Reiko's thigh under the table again. A settled happiness washed away her rage. "The beauty of having been friends for a long time before we…" Yolande paused.

"Formed a closer relationship." Reiko filled in the gap with the perfect phrasing, and it reminded Yolande that they were seated at a wedding dinner with a bunch of other people doing their best to pretend they weren't eavesdropping. Oh God, the rush of emotion twisted and changed like a stormy sea, raging in the wind, and full of changing colours as the waves rose and fell under a shifting sky. So dramatic, and it gave her an idea for a new burlesque routine. Ace would make the most glorious costume for that idea. Later. She tucked the idea away until she had space to focus on it.

With a deep breath, she gave Mr Inoue an honest answer. "Yes. The best part of being friends first is that we already talk to each other about all sorts of things, so when Reiko mentioned your business and all that came with it, it was a surprise because Reiko had never given me any reason to…" Yolande wasn't sure how to go on without insulting Reiko's parents inadvertently. What if they were upset that Reiko had never mentioned them? "Anyway, I might have blurted out something about her holding back on me, but once I understood how often people treated her differently once they learn about you, then it was easy to empathise with her choice to keep that information to herself." Yolande shrugged. "It took me no time at all to see it as a necessary protective measure for Reiko against the sharks of the world."

"I understand." Mr Inoue considered her with a long look, and Yolande tried not to buckle under the pressure of his stare.

"Father, leave Yolande alone. If she's only with me for the money, I will find that out in time, and I'll only have myself to blame for falling for the same old tricks again." Reiko got right to the point that they'd all been mincing around. It was actually kind of sweet that Mr Inoue cared that Reiko wasn't getting herself into a relationship where she'd get hurt by a gold digger. It almost made up for the pile of comments he'd previously made that implied he was disappointed by her. Almost.

"I'm worried, that's all."

"I know, Father. Thank you."

Yolande allowed the family banter to wash over her, relieved that Mr Inoue seemed to be content with her answers. If she wasn't so upset with Helen for taking her crystal, she'd be inclined to see the coincidence of having the crystal in the room as the reason that this conversation—which could easily have gone south—turned out well enough. Her lucky crystal still worked for her, even when it was hanging around someone else's neck.

"Reiko is lucky to have a family who cares deeply for her." Maybe she laid that one on a little thickly because Reiko squeezed her thigh a lot tighter.

"Poor Yolande had a nasty surprise when we arrived. The staff informed me that you were here, and unfortunately she thought they meant her parents."

"Only for a second. It sounds ridiculous now. I can only say that after a long drive and too much coffee, I stared at this whole incredible house, and assumed that my mother was back from the dead and wanted to have a drink with me." Hot tears speared her eyes; what she wouldn't give for one more day. One more day to tell her mum how much she appreciated her.

"Yolande, it's okay." Reiko brushed a gentle kiss to her cheek and held her hands tight.

Yolande swallowed. "I'm sorry. I don't understand why that happened."

"Grief is a complicated thing," Reiko paused. "When are they going to bring the dessert?"

Mrs Inoue smiled. "I'm so sorry to hear about your mother, Miss Cantor."

"Thank you. Please call me Yolande."

"Yolande. May I ask after your father?"

Yolande tried not to snort, but at least the question made her tears disappear. "Sure. I have no answers for you. I'm named after his mother and that's all I know. He left before I was born and I've had zero contact with him. Mum tried to get child support from him for years to no avail. He didn't even contact me when Mum died in a car accident. Nothing."

"Oh." Mrs Inoue stiffened in her chair.

"Was I too blunt? I have no interest in discussing him. He left Mum to raise me alone, but it was okay. She taught me the power of a strong woman. I admired my mum very much." Yolande had been gutted that night when she'd heard about her mum's accident. It was the one time she wished she wasn't a nurse, because when the paramedics described the accident site and said that her death had been quick, she'd known they were lying. Her mum had died in incredible pain, all thanks to a rainy night and not enough sleep. She'd worked herself literally to death, for Yolande.

When Reiko wiped her face with her napkin, Yolande blinked hard. Had she just burst into tears during a fancy wedding dinner? And the worst nasty little thought was that she really fucking hoped Helen didn't see, because she'd assume the tears were about her. If anything, all this flooding emotion made Yolande want to storm up there and rip her crystal off Helen's neck and leave this place forever. She breathed out. Yeah, that wasn't exactly a rational response.

"Come with me." Reiko stood up, and gently helped Yolande out of her chair. "Dessert can wait."

She let herself be guided out of the room, only vaguely aware that Reiko deliberately kept her out of people's view.

13

———

"I'm so sorry." Reiko couldn't believe where this conversation was going. Firstly Father actually quizzed Yolande on whether she only cared for their money, which was both great because she had been worried about that herself and also totally embarrassing for her father to bring it up at a public dinner with people eavesdropping. Reiko had already decided that Yolande was more upset at Reiko not telling the truth than she cared about Father's money. But none of that mattered. She'd upset Yolande with her throwaway memory of Yolande's reaction when they'd arrived here. God, she felt like such a fool. Why bring that up? It had obviously opened up a raw wound, given the tears streaming down Yolande's face. Tears that were completely her fault. What a terrible friend she was.

"I shouldn't have mentioned your mum."

"It's okay. It's nice to think about her sometimes."

Reiko nodded. "I remember her. She used to come to your shows sometimes."

"She did. She didn't understand why I wanted to dance naked. Why couldn't I do ballet or jazz or something more savoury? But she always supported me." Yolande swallowed, and a hesitant grin slowly emerged from under the tears. "I'm sorry. I'm not usually a watering pot."

"It's fine. Really. Come into the bathroom here and get cleaned up." She opened up the door to the small washroom near the ballroom, and guided Yolande inside. "Do you want me to run up to our room to grab your makeup?"

Reiko needed to do something useful to help after causing Yolande's tears. She was good at helping people, it was her favourite thing, to rush about doing things for people, to show she cared. Love in action. She gulped and tried not to sway as she felt oddly light-headed.

"No, it's fine. Look, I'll just dab here and there and it'll be okay."

"If you are certain?" Because Reiko wasn't at all certain. She had thought herself to be in love with Yolande for years, always admiring her, lusting after her body and her self-assured confidence, and her laugh. Fuck, she loved her laugh. But this… this tempest of sensation taking over her body was more than a theoretical love. Suddenly, she doubted her old love for Yolande. She wasn't at all certain that what she'd felt before was love. Because this—this need to fix her mistakes and care for Yolande—was greater than a vague notion of love. She was actually in love in Yolande. Sex had changed everything.

No. It had deepened everything and made her earlier feelings real. Tangible.

"Yes. Fuck." Yolande's vehement swear cut into her heart.

Had Yolande heard her thoughts? Had she said all that stuff out loud. Her stomach dropped and she stepped away, her throat thick.

"Sorry, do you want me to back off?"

"No. What?" Yolande's face twisted in a frown. "This has been a lot, that's all."

"The wedding?" Obviously the wedding. Reiko would've rolled her eyes if she'd been alone and no one could see her annoyance at herself. Stop bloody thinking so selfishly and think about Yolande's perspective. It had to be incredibly difficult for Yolande to watch Helen marry someone else.

"Well, yeah, but I meant tonight's dinner specifically."

"Oh?"

Yolande finished dabbing her left eye and scrunched up the tissue before letting out a huge sigh. "Fucking hell. Where do I start?"

"The beginning?" Could she get any more awkward? Far out. Just as the spiral of negative thoughts started, Reiko felt Yolande bump her with her hip.

"Reiko!" Yolande's rumble of laughter wasn't much but the noise gave Reiko a little hope that she wasn't overcome with grief, that Reiko hadn't completely messed this all up.

"Well?"

"Fine. We walked into dinner after some truly amazing sex. Fuck, my legs were still like jelly as we walked down the main stairs—"

Reiko's cheeks warmed. She'd poured her heart into every touch of Yolande's skin and to hear that Yolande had adored the attention was the cat's pyjamas. It was the perfect thank you for her outpouring of love and care.

"—and the food has been… Wow. But—" Yolande

wiped her other eye and Reiko waited for her, trying not to stress about 'but what?' Yolande threw her tissue down on the sink bench and Reiko couldn't help herself. She picked up the balled up tissues and threw them into the bin.

"The way everyone brown-nosed you and your mother, using you as obvious stepping stones, really started to piss me off more and more during dinner. And I might not be rich, or understand how that feels to you, but I think I get it. It's the same thing Helen did to me."

"Right. I thought you looked upset or angry during the beef course."

Yolande stretched out her limbs in a typical dancer's pose, rather like a cat preparing to pounce. "Yes. But it wasn't just that. I'm so bloody angry."

"About?" Reiko pinched the bridge of her nose. Was Yolande still talking about Reiko's parents?

"Fucking Helen is wearing my lucky blue lace agate crystal."

"Tonight?" What the hell! Reiko's breath stalled in her mouth and she dropped her hands to her hips.

"Yes, tonight. And yes, I'm completely sure that it's mine."

"I believe you. I remember it was missing that night." The night Helen had dumped Yolande with no notice. Reiko blew out a long breath. "I find it somewhat audacious that she was too cowardly to break up with you in person, using Beth to do it, and then have the fucking balls to wear a stolen crystal… your crystal to dinner tonight."

"Yes. I've already fantasised about marching up there and ripping it off her."

Reiko wanted to see that, even though they couldn't. She

stood beside Yolande, fuming with every breath of air. It took a while to calm the unsteady thump of her heart and the way her veins burned with pulsing blood.

"I have a better idea." A vague unformed plan started to reveal itself, rather like a dancer peeling off a long skirt.

"Please. Anything is better than sitting there stewing in rage."

Reiko huffed out a strangled laugh unable to stop herself because she'd been raging internally too. "There's no need for that. A simple quiet plan is always better than fuming."

"Don't people always say that it's always the quiet ones you have to watch, and I reckon you are about to prove them right, aren't you?"

"Maybe?" Reiko didn't like the idea that she was always… "I'm not a natural schemer, so this might not work. And it's kind of… brazen?"

"Brazen?"

"Yeah. Um, I thought we'd wait until the dancing, and then cut in and dance with her. You slide behind her and undo the necklace, and I'll grab it when it drops, then we'll bolt before she notices."

Yolande shook her head. "That's not brazen at all. Brazen would be for me to dance with her, for one last goodbye or something. I'll make something up. Then I'll mention the crystal, as you undo it. It'll drop into my hand. I'll thank her for returning the crystal to me after she borrowed it. Then we'll bolt."

"What if she freaks out?"

"It's her wedding," Yolande threw out that titbit as if it explained everything. Reiko ran her tongue across her teeth, and tried to figure out what that meant and why wasn't Yolande more worried about what Helen would do?

"I'm not overly comfortable with this." The plan put Yolande right in the firing line if Helen argued with them. "It relies on Helen not crying thief…"

"At her own wedding? Nah. She hates confrontation." Yolande spat out those words with such bitterness.

Oh. Suddenly Reiko understood. Yolande still hadn't completely come to terms with the way Helen had dumped her. Could they make their new relationship work with that pain sitting between them? On a long intake of breath, she pushed away that worry. There were more immediate things to stress about and deal with, like getting Yolande's crystal returned to her.

"Let's go. It's time to receive some stolen property."

Yolande giggled. "What? That's not what we are doing. Receiving stolen property is when someone knicks something then sells it to someone else. We are going on a heist to get my crystal back from the person who stole it."

"A heist. I like that. It sounds positively criminal." Reiko had never broken the law in her life, which she knew was a little ironic given that successful business people continually blurred the lines of the law. On the other hand, many laws, like the anti-queer ones, were bad laws and deserved to be broken. This train of thought wasn't particularly practical or useful. She rubbed her temples.

Yolande reached up and held her hands, pulling them away from her face. "Reiko. It's more that we are righting a wrong done against us."

"Civil justice."

Yolande rolled her eyes. "Sure, whatever. This was basically your idea anyway, so I don't know why you are suddenly having ethical qualms about it."

"Ideas are one thing. Implementation is quite another."

"Don't lose your nerve now. I want my lucky crystal back. And I'll do it alone if you chicken out." Yolande dropped Reiko's hands. Just as Reiko was about to leave the bathroom and get ready to do a heist—a heist!—Yolande reached up and straightened the neckline on Reiko's dress. She fussed with the fabric, brushing it down, and smoothing out all the little wrinkles. Each touch sent a little vibration scattering across Reiko's skin, and her nipples reacted by pinching tight. Almost immediately, Reiko's body was ready to grind against Yolande; heist and other dramas forgotten as heat surged.

"Come on then. Let's do this." Yolande spun around, leaving Reiko needing more.

Yolande shook her head, her eyes now dry and clear, as she stepped out into the hallway. Who would have picked Reiko as someone who could come up with such a plan? A plan that was basically: march up to Helen and demand the necklace back. It was everything Yolande desperately wanted to do, and it amused her that Reiko would suggest the plan, then think way too hard about the ethics of going through with it.

This whole evening had been fucking trippy; a mess of tangled emotions. And now she was about to take back control over her life from Helen. Their entire relationship had been defined by Yolande always submitting to whatever whim Helen had. The only thing she'd stood strong on was not getting a puppy, and she probably only won that one because Helen loved the idea of a puppy but didn't actually want to commit.

It was time to get her crystal back and show Helen—and herself—that she'd moved on. She wanted a relationship on a fairer footing. She wanted Reiko in all her complicated glory, in all her guises. She wanted to be the shoulder Reiko rested on when her parents got a little overbearing, and the person that Reiko went home from Seraph's with after a long evening entertaining people. She wanted to be the person who supported Reiko when she was exhausted from caring for everyone else; the one who cared for Reiko with the same energy Reiko expended on her.

"Try to look a little more relaxed. You've only just left the room crying." Reiko nudged Yolande gently.

"Right. Of course." Yolande had almost forgotten about that, caught up in the anticipation of confronting Helen and getting her crystal back. It all flooded back on a hiccuppy breath. Shit.

"You look magnificent. Like a warrior about to go into battle, all tall and upright and fierce." Reiko's throaty comment almost stopped Yolande dead in her tracks.

Was Reiko turned on by this? Hopefully. Because Yolande knew how to deal with that—sex was something she understood. A place she took control over her life; it was why she loved burlesque, it gave her power, a way of commanding a room and controlling the way people saw her. She loved the anticipation of it, the way her blood heated and her skin warmed. She loved seeing people react to her and the intimate moments of sex were the same, the teasing of foreplay, and most especially, she adored discovering what made someone else feel good.

"Umm." Yolande couldn't cope with the competing emotions fizzing in her blood. Lust. Anger. Sadness. Need. Desire. Power. Reiko's view of her as a warrior about to conquer her nemesis and get her crystal back was so fucking hot.

"Just relax. Have some dessert."

"Okay. Lead the away." Yolande let Reiko guide her back to the table and she sat down, making sure she didn't glance over at Helen.

Mrs Inoue reached across the table and patted Yolande's hand. "Are you feeling better?"

"Yes. Thank you for asking."

"I understand. Grief is very sneaky."

Yolande swallowed the fresh lump in her throat. "It is. I'm usually okay about it, but sometimes it—"

"Just surprises." Mrs Inoue showed traces of Reiko's empathy in her voice.

"Yes. I hope I didn't interrupt anything." Or break some other piece of etiquette.

"No. We were very concerned, that's all."

"Oh. Thank you. That's very kind of you." Yolande was glad for the boring polite conversation as it prevented her from thinking too hard about Reiko's heist plan. They really hadn't discussed enough details about this and the longer she had to wait, the more impossible the idea seemed. When Reiko had first mentioned it, she'd been ready to pounce.

"You missed a few of the speeches, but no matter. The Earl of Gattingly was eloquent as usual," Mr Inoue said. A group of waiters came past with the dessert offering: zeppole filled with ricotta and a strawberry and rhubarb compote. The little donuts looked decadent and each one had B&H, Brian and Helen, stencilled on them in icing sugar. Yolande couldn't wait to try them; although the initials were super weird. If she were alone with Reiko, she would lick off the icing sugar stencils and banish Helen from her life forever. Focus, damn it. Now wasn't the time to think about how freaking weird it was to eat Helen's initial. The donuts were paired with a splash of gin on the rocks in a beautiful glass tumbler. Rich people's livers must be well preserved if this was how they ate and drank regularly. During the dessert, the best man gave a speech that was mostly in-jokes from whatever fancy school he'd gone to with Brian. Yolande was grateful for it, as she could focus on eating the dessert and trying to school her unsteady heartbeat into a regular pattern.

Having Reiko seated next to her didn't help, because every glance sideways at her, and every time Reiko moved, all Yolande could hear was the way Reiko's dress shifted on her skin. In movies, this moment was always shown with only the couple, with the background faded away. It'd never made sense, except as a silly overrepresentation of lust, until now. It felt just like that; all her senses were heightened around Reiko and nothing else in the room existed.

The dessert tasted like nothing because all she could smell was Reiko's perfume. Conversations faded to background noise, and all she could hear was the rhythm of Reiko's breath and the way her dress rustled slightly as she lifted her fork to her mouth. Yolande forced herself not to stare at Reiko's lips as she ate a tiny slice of donut. If she focused her gaze on her own plate, maybe no one would notice that Yolande was flushed with lust. Or anticipation. Perhaps they were the same thing. She stayed like that, just listening to Reiko, for an unknown amount of time, until Reiko touched her on the shoulder. A spark flew from her shoulder across her throat and spread over her body. Did warrior women get wet like this before battle?

"Yes?" Yolande's voice was all sharp and high pitched. She cleared her throat. "Is it time now?"

"Not yet. The dancing is about to start, so we should say hi to Anne." Reiko stood up and said something blandly polite to the other people sitting at their table. It didn't really sink in because Yolande was torn between dragging Reiko to bed and needing everyone to hurry up and dance so she could get her lucky crystal back.

"In the movies, the characters look so calm before a heist. How? My pulse is racing," Reiko whispered, adding to Yolande's scattered thoughts.

"So is mine. Are we certain we want to do this?"

Reiko shrugged. "No. But yes. I can't think of any other way to get your crystal back without a fuss. If we approach her in private, she could easily say no. This way, she has to either comply or make a fuss and you said she wouldn't do that."

"Okay. Okay. Cool. Cool." Yolande breathed in. They could do this. It'd be a lot easier if they fucked first to take the edge of her racing pulse. Fuck.

"Breathe. Slowly."

Yolande scoffed at Reiko's soothing tone. "How are you not nervous about this?"

"I am. I'm just good at hiding it, while you are all flushed and your leg is shaking."

Yolande rolled her neck on her shoulders and stretched out her arms. "Thanks a lot."

"For?"

"Pointing out that I don't look composed."

"Would you rather I lied to you?" Reiko frowned, while somehow guiding her to the edge of the room away from the crowds who were shifting towards the back of the ballroom where the band was set up. People started to clap, and Yolande twisted. Oh. Helen and Brian were walking down the centre of the room, between tables towards the dance floor and people were applauding their progress. Yolande leaned back against a concrete pillar.

"No. Don't lie to me." She didn't think she could stand it if Reiko did that. "I'd rather have the ugly truth and the confrontation." It was what Helen had always avoided and in the end it was better that Helen had walked away from her if she couldn't be fucking honest. Okay... Yolande breathed out. It was going to take some time to stop feeling hurt and angry by Helen's actions; not just the way she had dumped Yolande, but the whole mess of their relationship. Maybe she could see the therapist at work and talk about it. Since the pandemic, the hospital had provided free therapy sessions for all the employees as a way of helping everyone try and cope with the loss of so many colleagues. She gulped. *Thanks a fucking lot brain.* She didn't need any extra reasons to get upset tonight. There had already been so many. Why was it that heightened emotions seemed to grow, like an out of control house fire, consuming everything around it?

"Okay." Yolande lifted her chin, ready for battle. "It's time to take charge of my life and get my lucky crystal back.

I need the wisdom, kindness, and honest energy that it provides." A frown flashed over Reiko's face. Yolande shook out her hands. "For me. You are already wise and kind and honest with me. I want that energy for the whole of my life and the crystal represents that."

14

———

"Wait." Reiko ignored Yolande's chatter about honesty. She was really worried about the way Yolande looked, as if she were going to push through the crowd, rip the crystal off Helen's neck, and punch her in the face. It was obvious to Reiko that Yolande only rambled on about the crystal because she was nervous and angry. Reiko could help by distracting her from their heist for a little while.

"What?" Yolande's terse bark reassured Reiko that she was on the correct path.

"I need to take a few photos of the room and send them to the Seraph's chat."

"Now? Seriously?" Yolande glared at her, and Reiko tried not to flinch under the powerful stare as Yolande's brown eyes blazed with intensity.

"Yes. Now." She needed to fill in a little time while Brian and Helen had their wedding dance. They couldn't do this heist at the beginning of the dancing; too many people would be focused on Helen, hence trying to delay Yolande for a moment. She pulled out her phone and flicked open the app.

"What are you doing?"

"Reading everyone's comments. Look at what Ace said about Satoko RK dress."

"Reiko." The sharp warning in Yolande's tone made Reiko gulp.

"Yes?"

"Let's just get this done, shall we?"

Reiko needed to delay Yolande for maybe two more songs. The string quartet had just begun playing a new song —was that Taylor Swift? The upbeat pop tune sounded great on those instruments. How was she going to distract Yolande for a little bit longer?

"How about we say hi to Anne, and then dance together first?"

"Are you backing down now?"

"No. Not at all. I just think we need to have a little strategy in this crowd. We can't just march up to her, other people might get upset and say something."

Yolande nodded. "Right. Just because Helen won't like confrontation, doesn't mean that others in the room will have no issues with us. We need to be a little bit subtle. Fuck."

"Fuck?"

"Yeah. I really want to just rip it off her. I can't believe she would do that, and the longer she wears it, the angrier I get."

Reiko hummed under her breath. "Consider this. Do you want your crystal, or do you want emotional satisfaction?"

"Can't I have both?"

"Not if satisfaction only comes with an angry gesture."

Yolande breathed in, the air whistling between her teeth, and Reiko waited until Yolande blew the air out again. "Fine. Let's get my crystal without a confrontation."

"Remember, it's a heist, not a punch up." Reiko tried to joke, but given the look on Yolande's face, it fell flat.

"Yeah. Come and dance." Yolande threw her arm around Reiko's waist and dragged her onto the dancefloor. Heat seared Reiko's back at Yolande's touch, but she had no time to adjust as Yolande marched through the crowd. Reiko wanted to lean her weight against Yolande's arm to slow her down, anything to stop the long strides, but given the way she was at risk of tripping over, she focused on walking beside Yolande in a way that hopefully looked natural. She placed her hand on top of Yolande's and squeezed it gently.

"I'm going too fast, aren't I?"

"Yes." There was no point in trying to protect Yolande by fudging the truth. "Let the crowds join the dancefloor first, so we have cover."

"Right." Yolande slowed down, her steps suddenly deliberate. "Dance training comes in handy sometimes, huh."

"Okay?" Reiko wasn't sure what that meant.

"It means—" Yolande's grip tightened around Reiko's waist, then relaxed again. "—it means I can move slowly even when I want to rush. All those years dancing on stage at Seraph's has taught me how to move in a rhythm, regardless of how I feel inside."

"You just tell yourself to go slowly, and you will?" Reiko had never really given much thought to the idea of muscle control, mostly because she'd never needed to know that skill. There was no way she'd ever get up on stage. Whenever Charlie gave her a shoutout during a show, she always ducked her head and tried to make herself invisible. She'd eventually learned to give a little wave to the crowd, but still hadn't been able to look at them.

"Yes. Now, let's dance."

"And find some cover. No marching up to Helen and demanding anything. We have to be subtle." Reiko allowed herself to be led onto the dance floor by Yolande, who swung her around into her arms, and swayed in time to the music. In any other circumstances, Reiko would have closed her eyes and allowed the music and Yolande's touch to surround her. Damn Helen for taking that moment away from her.

"Relax. Fuck, you are so stiff." Yolande linked the fingers on her left hand through Reiko's, resting their palms together. Reiko tried to relax, breathing out slowly. As soon as she almost managed some semblance of relaxation, someone nudged her in the back.

"Sorry." She couldn't help herself, even though it wasn't her fault. The person moved on.

"How rude. That was totally their fault." Yolande whispered and Reiko grinned at the way she sounded so affronted by someone bumping into her.

"It's fine. And the upside is—"

"How is there an upside to being pushed by someone?"

"The dancefloor is crowded, which means…" Reiko paused, not wanting to mention their heist plans aloud.

"Okay. I'll thread us through the crowd."

"In a zig-zag. No marching up to her. At least try—"

"And make it subtle. I know, I know."

Reiko chuckled. "You didn't have to interrupt me." Her laughter extended as she actually stood up for herself and told Yolande off.

"I'm sorry. I tend to talk over people when I get nervous. Am I being really annoying?"

"No. It's fine." It wasn't really, but Yolande's explanation made sense and Reiko didn't want to dwell on it anyway. Not when she needed to focus on what was about to happen. What they were about to do. Fuck. She eased out a long sigh.

"I take it that sigh means it's not really fine." Yolande raised one eyebrow, as she seamlessly moved them between two other couples.

"Yes, talking over me is quite annoying." Reiko opted for the truth.

"Have I made a mess of everything?"

"No. What?" Reiko wished she had more practice at relationships because she was more confused than ever.

"Okay. Sorry, I'm just really nervous and I don't want to… Never mind." Yolande breathed in sharply and spun Reiko around unexpectedly. She stumbled, and her heart skipped a beat as she tried to keep her footing, only to find herself staring at Helen.

"Hi Helen. Great wedding. Congratulations." *Wow, good work, Reiko.* Way to show Helen that she was nervous about their planned heist.

"Thanks, Reiko. Yolande, have you enjoyed yourself?"

"It's been interesting, that's for sure." Yolande didn't answer Helen's question and a flush of colour splashed on Helen's cheeks before disappearing again. Reiko slipped out of Yolande's hold and moved away from her. Hopefully

Helen wouldn't notice her; after all she hadn't for years at Seraph's. It did her no credit to have such mean petty thoughts; she knew how they felt when aimed at her and she'd worked hard not to throw them at other people. But this was Helen, whose cowardly break up was only the one of the many ways she'd badly treated Yolande.

"Speaking of interesting, that's an interesting crystal you are wearing tonight. I'm sure I've seen it somewhere before."

Reiko swallowed back a choked laugh and kept moving so she stood close enough to Helen to undo the necklace. Thankfully the crystal was on a long chain that had a normal clip at the back of Helen's neck.

"It's my something blue." Helen's voice didn't change, didn't show any sign that she was discussing a crystal that she stole. "You know the old saying—something old, something new, something borrowed, something blue…"

"And you just thought you could take it?"

"Ah, yes, well, I was going to tell you, but I've been so busy with the wedding preparations and everything."

Reiko rolled her eyes at Helen's nonsense and focused on lifting the chain a little off Helen's neck so she could access the clip.

Helen didn't seem to notice. "I thought you wouldn't mind because the crystal was for both of us, for good luck."

"It is my crystal, not ours. And besides, when people split up, they discuss how to split shared property, they don't just take it. You didn't borrow it—" Yolande started to wind up and Reiko knew this was her moment.

"It won't do you any good, Helen," Reiko said. She quickly undid the chain and it dropped. Reiko wasn't tall enough to see over Helen's shoulder, so she had to hope

Yolande caught it. Reiko held her breath as she waited for the clunk as the crystal hit the ground. She didn't hear anything.

"Why not?" Helen asked. *Because stealing is wrong, obviously.* Reiko's palms were clammy, and she moved away from Helen's back and stood beside Yolande.

"You are supposed to borrow something from a happily married woman who has lots of children, to bless your marriage with fertility." Yolande's voice had a little squeak of excitement. "Borrowing it from me, especially without telling me, isn't going to meet the intention of the rhyme."

"Does that mean that each part of the rhyme has a meaning?" Helen asked.

"No. The new means nothing, but the blue is intended to ward off the evil eye. Congratulations on your marriage, Helen. I hope you find happiness." Yolande spun away from Helen, and Reiko took that as her cue to fade backwards into the crowd. It wasn't until she'd made her way to the side of the room that she caught up to Yolande.

"I've got it." The grin on Yolande's face was worth the risk of grabbing it from Helen. The way her smile lit up her face sent a warm flutter into Reiko's torso.

"Awesome. Let's get out of here." Reiko quickly glanced around the room but didn't see her parents, so she headed towards the end of the ballroom.

"Yes!" Yolande paced past her, and together they left the room, trying and failing to walk slowly. As soon as they were out of the ballroom, Reiko laughed.

"We did it."

"We did." Yolande held out her hand with the crystal lying on her palm.

Reiko closed her hand over it briefly, then let go again.

"Come on." She paced towards the stairs and rushed to their room. Yolande's lips covered hers as they tumbled inside, and it was only then that their laughter stopped. It still bubbled inside Reiko, fuelling their kiss with a joy and post-heist release. She wanted to share this glee. Her whole body felt light and her skin on fire with excitement.

She broke the kiss on a gasp of air. "No wonder people turn to crime if this is the adrenalin rush they get."

"Crime? What are you talking about? This feels good because we've returned my crystal to its rightful owner."

"You?" Reiko laughed.

"Yes, me." Yolande kissed her again, and the kiss deepened easily with the now familiar connection. Wow. Reiko could get used to kissing Yolande like this every day. The taste of her blended with the strawberry and rhubarb from the wedding dessert, creating a lush sweetness that was, well, moreish.

"Unzip me," Yolande murmured against Reiko's neck, nuzzling in. When Reiko nodded, Yolande closed her mouth over the tendon above Reiko's collarbone and sucked. The rush of heat from Yolande's scalding mouth sizzled down Reiko's torso directly into her already soaked underwear. Reiko needed to get her skin against Yolande's so the command was already being answered as Yolande spoke it. She slid Yolande's dress down over her shoulders, letting it float down her body, then reached under her left arm to unzip herself. Her own dress—the antique Gucci gown— was delicate and she ought to be careful. It was difficult to focus on ensuring the embroidered fabric didn't snag given the way Yolande's touch stole away her brain power.

"Wait a second." She needed a little bit of space to work out the logistics of her gown.

Yolande immediately stepped backwards, her own dress falling around her feet, leaving her to stand before Reiko wearing only her lingerie. Reiko gulped; would she ever get used to seeing Yolande like this? It was so different to when Yolande danced—that was hot but in a distant way—this was so intimate and personal and just for her. Reiko licked her lips, then blinked. She went through the motions quickly, then hung the gown carefully over the back of a chair. It could be hung properly later.

"Hold on. Did you just stop us so you could put your gown away?"

Reiko shrugged. "It's not away, just cared for." She bent down and picked up Yolande's gown and shook it out gently to do the same.

"Sure. Mine doesn't need the same care. It's literally a no-brand name off the rack gown that I got on sale a couple of years ago."

"Price doesn't matter. Objects should be looked after, and then they will last." Reiko lay Yolande's gown over hers on the same chair.

"Come here."

Reiko straightened only to gasp once again. Yolande lay on the bed, with her legs crossed, posing just for her. In a few strides, she bounded over and crawled onto the bed, sliding her hands up Yolande's smooth long legs. The energy from their successful heist zipped around her body and she moved her hands everywhere, caressing Yolande's gorgeous lean dancer's body.

Yolande was no passive partner in this dance, and Reiko

soon found herself rolled underneath Yolande with the soft linen bed cover against her back as Yolande pressed her into the bed. A frantic, slightly chaotic, air filled the room as they both explored with hands and tongues and teeth.

Reiko kissed every part of Yolande that she could reach, gripping to her spine with one hand, and trying to explore her tits with the other. She ended up with her hand squashed between them both, unable to move. Just as she almost groaned with frustration, Yolande rolled them both onto their sides.

"Ahh, that's better." Reiko kissed Yolande again, before covering both of her tits with her hands. Yolande's nipples were hard under her palms, and she made easy work of playing with them until Yolande moaned into her mouth. The vibration traversed through her, and when Yolande pressed her leg between Reiko's, she spread her legs. Ready. More than ready. Desperate for Yolande's touch there, where she was wet.

"Why didn't we undress properly?" Yolande whispered against Reiko's cheek as her fingers dove under Reiko's lingerie. As they slipped into her folds, she cried out.

"I would like to see you bare for me," Yolande said.

"God. Next time. Please." Reiko had been ready for Yolande ever since undoing the clasp on the chain holding Yolande's crystal around Helen's neck. She arched her back, pressing her sex against Yolande's hand. Yolande kept her hand still, a heavy presence with her fingers almost pressed inside her, and with her other hand, Yolande covered Reiko's own hand and pulled it lower down Yolande's body. Reiko needed no more encouragement and slipped her hand inside Yolande's gorgeous lace lingerie. That first touch of her silky folds and the discovery that Yolande was as wet as she was had her panting for breath. She used her fingers to play with Yolande, toying with her clit until Yolande responded in the very best way by filling Reiko with her own fingers.

"Purr for me, little kitty."

From anyone else, it would've pissed Reiko right off, but when Yolande said it in that husky voice filled with desire, Reiko could do nothing else but moan. Yolande's skilled fingers had her purring just as she was told. All she could do was copy Yolande's motions, and when Yolande kissed her again and pressed deeper inside her, the rush of heat and build up of pressure was almost too much to take.

"Your pussy is so beautiful." Yolande nipped at Reiko's earlobe. She jerked at the tiny shock of pain, pushing her thumb hard against Yolande's clit.

"More?"

How could Yolande even talk right now? Reiko could do nothing more than react.

"More?" Yolande asked again as she relaxed her hand, removing some of the delicious pressure.

"Please." Reiko showed Yolande what she wanted, flicking her clit with her thumb, and the resulting groan was worth it. Yolande almost let up with her own movements, but quickly they found a rhythm together and soon Reiko could do nothing but cling to Yolande's body as she came in a wild rush.

The entirety of the night, all the excitement and antici-pation yielded to a climax that rumbled and exploded through her body with a release of pressure that was perfectly delicious. Yolande kissed her deeply, and all Reiko could taste was Yolande's signature essence with the hint of strawberry and rhubarb from dessert, as Yolande also came, the two of them moaning into each other's mouths as their bodies clenched and released in unison.

"Fucking hell. What a night." Yolande lay next to Reiko, half draped across her, her fingers still inside her. "I can't believe we did that and got away with it."

Reiko nodded her agreement, managing to press one last kiss to Yolande's cheek. Hopefully they would still be successful heist winners tomorrow. Heisters? Heist-doers? Whatever. The sheer wildness of the night and the adrenalin buzz that turned into a brilliant orgasm had her unable to do anything but close her eyes and drift away into a sated sleep.

15

Yolande's glow from the wedding hadn't faded even a week after being back at work. On the drive home from Rutheringholme, Yolande and Reiko had talked and laughed and kissed—yes, they'd stopped off for lunch on the way, ending up fucking each other in the laneway behind the restaurant, hidden from view—and it'd been amazing. Launching right back into night shift after arriving in London would normally have ruined Yolande's temper, but she was too happy to care. She usually hated the disconnecting way her body felt after a night shift when she tried to sleep with the light of day.

Most of Yolande's colleagues had teased her about how the weekend away had done her good, although most of them didn't go as far as to ask her about whether she'd gotten laid. It was probably obvious from the way she couldn't stop humming under her breath, and randomly grinning all the time.

Since she had dropped Reiko off outside an intimidatingly expensive apartment building a week ago, they hadn't found time to see each other. Yolande didn't mind, even though she missed Reiko's touch and her smile, because she needed time to work out her life. She hadn't expected to fall into a new relationship only a few months after the last mess.

Having been friends for a long time before they'd had sex helped ease a lot of Yolande's concerns, and the other thing that helped was the way Reiko surprised her every morning after her night shift with a phone call. Reiko was always awake at the ungodly early hour and willing to chat as Yolande drove home. When she'd asked, Reiko had merely said that of course she would keep her company as she drove, as if she had nothing else to do. To be prioritised like that was really special and pushed away Yolande's doubts about her readiness regarding stepping into a new relationship.

Finally, after a week apart, Yolande was going to see Reiko for lunch today. Her rostered night shifts had ended early this morning, she'd chatted to Reiko on her drive home, then slept deeply. Being cared for in Reiko's subtle way really eased her anxiety around driving home after work. Not many people knew she suffered from anxiety. She literally used burlesque to overcome it, because it forced her into the spotlight where she was in control of the tease and the way people saw her. Somehow Reiko knew, without Yolande really saying anything. Reiko listened—properly listened— to her. She'd heard the story of how her mum had died in a car crash while driving home from work, tired, and she'd made sure that Yolande had someone to talk to and keep her awake and safe as she drove home after each night shift.

In a few minutes, Reiko would be here. Yolande probably should tell her that she was grateful and to thank her for caring. Why was that hard to do?

This last week, being back in her apartment had been quite weird. She hadn't really realised how strange it was to live there without Helen, and how much of Helen's presence still lingered about the place. If it wasn't for Captain and Bounce, she'd already be looking for a different place that would give her a fresh start. She'd sent a text to Reiko saying as much a couple of days ago.

"Bounce. Will you stop destroying the couch?" The kitten had decided the couch was a much better scratching post than the one Yolande had bought specifically for that purpose. She picked up the kitten and cuddled him, and he immediately relaxed in her arms and began to purr. "You are such a softy, aren't you?"

Captain glanced over, then went back to licking his foot. "And you, you grumpy old thing." He was still mad at her for leaving him with Steph and Walter for a few days while she had gone to the wedding. It was pretty bad timing as he'd taken a long time to trust her, and then she'd rushed away and left him. Poor thing. Being on night shift for a week probably hadn't helped either.

"Your best friend Reiko will be here soon." At her name, he shifted slightly, as if he wanted to look excited but wasn't sure he could trust the news. She stroked Bounce along his spine, wandering aimlessly around her small apartment. She really should move. Not just move out of this apartment, but also move on from her old relationship. A new place would help her embrace the new her. She could find somewhere that she actually liked; somewhere up high, with a view and a balcony. There weren't many nice summer evenings in London, but there were enough that having a balcony to sit on and watch the sunset over the city would be magical. Helen had wanted a ground floor unit and Yolande had just gone along with it.

"Why can't I stop?" she grumbled at Bounce. If she was going to move on, either alone or with Reiko, she had to stop regretting her old decisions. From now on, she would decide what she wanted. Finally, there was a knock at the door. She rushed over to open it.

"Reiko. It's so good to see you."

Reiko beamed and stepped inside, pulling the door closed behind her. "I've missed you."

Yolande thought she was going to lean in for a kiss, but she patted Bounce instead.

"You've missed me or the cats?"

"Both." Reiko scratched Bounce behind his ears and his purring doubled in volume. "Speaking of which, where is Captain?"

"He's sulking in the lounge."

"Sulking?" Reiko frowned.

"I'm pretty sure he's mad at me for leaving him with Steph and Walter." Yolande walked into the lounge and grinned as Captain looked at her, then lifted up a different paw and licked it. He only had three to select from, and he'd rotated between cleaning them all for ages now. "He's been doing that all morning."

"Oh, you funny creature, Captain." Reiko didn't look at him. She just sat down on the couch. "What's the plan for lunch? Did you want to go out somewhere?"

Yolande stood in the middle of her small lounge, oddly uncertain. What did she want to do? She breathed in slowly.

Okay, she really wanted to drag Reiko to her bedroom and kiss her until they both moaned. A chuckle caught in her throat. Captain would be jealous. Well, she was jealous of him. Just as she'd been standing here, Captain had wandered over to Reiko and was winding himself around her legs.

"You two." She shook her head at the bond between Reiko and Captain. They'd been firm friends since they'd first met, and it should've been a sign that Reiko was more than a friend to her as well. Reiko always made Yolande feel cared for, and listened to, even when she didn't know what she wanted.

"We are both shy. It makes sense that we understand each other. Like you and Bounce. You both like to move, you love people, you like to perform."

Yolande grinned. "Very true."

Reiko dangled one hand down, and Captain brushed up against it. "Are you going to sit down?"

"Yeah, I guess."

"It is your place."

Yolande bit her bottom lip. "Yeah, it doesn't really feel like it anymore." She plonked herself down in a chair and crossed her legs. Bounce jumped onto her shoulder and curled his little body around her neck. For a kitten, he made a very heavy warm scarf.

"About that. I have a solution."

"Okay?" Yolande's brain computed what Reiko had said very slowly. Yolande obviously hadn't had enough sleep this week. *Solution? Solution? Oh.* It hit her with a gasp. Reiko was going to ask her to move in with her, wasn't she? Suddenly, Yolande didn't know if she would say yes. If she was to make her own decisions going forward, did she want to leap into something new without thinking it through first? She swallowed, annoyed at the bitter taste on her tongue. Before Helen, she'd been decisive. Before her mum had died and before the pandemic. When had she lost her natural ability to know what she wanted? Was it grief or some sort of PTSD? She didn't know, only that she might need more time to work it all out.

"My current apartment isn't cat friendly."

So… Reiko wasn't going to ask her to move in? Yolande held her breath. Was this disappointment or relief that swirled around her like a cool breeze against bare skin?

"I've bought a new apartment and I'm giving up my lease on my place." Reiko's statement still didn't include a solution.

"Okay…"

"And you sent me that text about not wanting to stay here, so I thought you and the cats would like to move in with me." Reiko's voice lowered to a whisper.

All her prior thoughts and worries fled for a second. Yolande wanted to say yes without second guessing herself; just follow her first instinct but she stopped herself.

"Let me think about it."

Reiko merely looked down at Captain and trailed her fingers along his furry back. He leaned against her and Yolande wanted to let go of her fear and say yes.

"Is it too fast?" Reiko whispered.

"Well, yeah. But also, you didn't talk to me first. All I sent was a text saying I didn't like this place and you've leaped into asking me to move in."

"I don't understand. I thought this would be a fun

surprise. I have the ownership documents and you are listed as an owner. I bought it for us."

Yolande shook her head at that. Yolande realised why Reiko's decision pissed her off. It was too close to how Helen had treated her; she'd always made decisions without bothering to find out Yolande's opinion, and this felt the same. How dare Reiko assume without asking? And do it for the both of them? No fucking way.

"Reiko. You can't be angry at people for treating you differently once they know you are rich, then behave like a rich kid by throwing your money around without consultation." Fuck. Of all the impulsive things that Reiko could have done, she'd literally bought a fucking house and put Yolande's name on the papers without asking. They'd never even discussed what type of architecture Yolande liked. Holy shit. As if that was the point right now.

"Oh."

"Yes. Oh." Yolande stood up and paced around the room. "We've literally had one weekend together and now you've bought us a fucking house without even asking me. Was this supposed to make me feel good?"

"Yes?"

"It doesn't."

"I see that." Reiko kept her head low.

"I… Fuck. Reiko, we had a really good time. I hope I didn't give you a reason to think this would work out in the long term." *Shut it, Yolande.* Fucking hell. She didn't want to break up with Reiko over this, but her mouth wouldn't stop. A little niggle tried to remind her that anger wasn't rational, but she didn't care to listen. What the fucking hell was this crap that Reiko had dropped at her feet?

Yolande wanted to be alone for a while to work out who the fuck she was when she wasn't going along with someone else's plans. Reiko hadn't just asked Yolande to move in with her; she'd bought a whole fucking house for them before even asking her if that was what she wanted. Reiko had literally just done to her exactly what Helen always did. How had Yolande been so foolish to end up in another relationship where she wasn't important enough for the other person to ask her opinion. She wanted her opinion to matter to her lover. Damn it.

"It was just one weekend. Not worth buying me a bloody house."

Reiko looked up, her cheeks flushed bright red. "I didn't buy you a house. I bought us a house."

"But it's not really for us if I didn't get a choice."

"Then we can buy a different one. Together, this time. You can pick."

Yolande's jaw was clenched so tight that her back teeth hurt. How fucking condescending.

"Fuck. You don't get it, do you? If you care so much about people not being with you for your money, then you shouldn't do things without their consent. I think you should go now."

The wedding weekend had been amazing, a surreal dream-like experience, and now Yolande realised that it wasn't real because Reiko didn't respect her enough to want her opinion.

"Okay." Reiko patted Captain and stood up. She walked out without another word, and once the door closed with a quiet click, Yolande collapsed back into her chair. Bounce protested by digging his claws in her thigh.

What had she done? She closed her eyes and heaved out a long sigh. She'd stood up for herself. That's what she'd done. How dare Reiko flash around her money without asking? Yolande was done with people deciding what she wanted. Yes, she didn't want to be in this apartment anymore; not with all the old memories and how they'd been tainted and changed by current events. Damn, she didn't want to even speak Helen's name anymore. That was over. She had her lucky crystal. She had Captain and Bounce. And most importantly, she had herself. She didn't need Reiko to rescue her. She had a good job and a decent regular income. It was all she needed to make her own choices. After pacing around the room for a while, she grabbed her phone and started to look up rental places.

It was time to solve her own problems and face an independent future. And she wasn't going to dwell on why that hurt so fucking much. Not at all. If Reiko couldn't listen to her, she'd rather be alone. She gulped back the lump in her throat and blinked away the rush of hot tears in her eyes. If she valued herself, then she couldn't be with someone who didn't ask for her opinion.

"Fuck you, Reiko. Why did you have to be so bloody perfect? And then do this to me?" She felt like the carpet had been ripped out from under her feet.

There was a tight clamp around her heart, desperately holding it together. In the last couple of months, she'd dealt with two break ups. One that she'd had no warning, and one that she'd instigated for her own protection. It was cold comfort, but it had to be enough. She'd done this for herself. If she said it often enough, she might eventually start believing it.

16

Reiko spent the next morning walking around London. She hadn't been able to sleep after the argument with Yolande; nothing had worked until eventually she got up and began walking. How could she have gotten it so wrong? She'd read and re-read Yolande's text about her apartment—the one that had spurred Reiko into buying them a place together. Yolande had said that she didn't want to live in that place with the hangover of Helen everywhere. Surely she'd been trying to say they should move in together. And it was just pragmatic to buy a place, so they didn't have to worry about landlords getting upset about Captain and Bounce. But it had gone completely wrong. She'd misunderstood the context, acted without asking, and now Yolande was really angry with her. Incredibly angry. And worst of all, Yolande was completely correct.

Her stomach rumbled and she glanced up. All her walking had taken her to Seraph's. Of course. How could her subconscious take her to the last place she wanted to be?

She didn't need a reminder of how much she'd fucked this up.

Across the road from Seraph's was a little sushi shop. She'd never been there because no sushi in London could beat what she'd eaten as a child in Japan; nothing was fresher than what her family's chef could prepare. She sat on the front step at Seraph's, staring at the evidence of her own snobbery, and held her head in her hands. Yolande was right, she was a little rich girl playing at life. She hated it when Father threw his money around and told her what to do. Why had she done the same thing to Yolande?

Caring about someone meant listening to them. It wasn't silently assuming what they wanted and doing it without asking. Without consent. Caring meant communication. If anyone should know that, it was her. She'd literally gone to therapy for years to understand this. How could she fuck this up so much? She'd let her excitement at wanting to help Yolande—and to be honest, the thrill of moving in with Yolande and making a life together—override good sense.

"Reiko?"

Reiko turned around to see Beth, Seraph's owner, leaning against the front door. "Hi."

"Are you alright?"

"Not really." She could admit that without having to talk about this whole mess, couldn't she?

"Come and have some sushi with me." Beth held the handrail as she walked down the steps. When Reiko had first started working at Seraph's, she had offered Beth her arm to assist her down the steps and had been firmly rebuked. Thankfully, Steph had taught her that if Beth wanted help, then she'd ask. It was ableist to assume that Beth automatically needed her help, just because she had a prosthetic limb. Beth was perfectly capable of knowing her own body. Reiko still felt a lingering guilt for the poor assumption, all these years later.

Having her brain remind her of past mistakes while she was in the midst of making another giant fuck-up was what she deserved. She ignored the cold inside her chest and resigned herself to terrible sushi instead. The dramatic notion nagged at her; in therapy, she'd learned that she tended to fall back on extreme thoughts when she was uncomfortable. Life wasn't all good or all bad; mostly it was somewhere in the middle. Messy and complicated.

"Okay." Hopefully the sushi would be ordinary, not terrible. She followed Beth across the road and into the small shop. When Beth sat down, Reiko slid onto the chair opposite.

"What do you want?" Beth handed her a menu and she glanced over it.

None of it really appealed. She avoided the fish options as they couldn't possibly be fresh enough for her snobbish upbringing. Sometimes acknowledging her privilege helped her remember that she didn't have the same perspective on the world as most people; that is, if she also tried to stop the negative cycle of thoughts that came with it. She didn't deserve her money, had done nothing to earn it, and only used it to hurt people.

Stop. She had to stop before she burst into tears. Pathetic. No one wanted to hear a rich kid cry because their expensive gift was rejected. Okay. She breathed out slowly. The spiral had begun. It was time to count her breaths and focus on five things. The table in front of her was cheap plastic. She ran her finger along it. It was clean and a tiny fragrant orange scent lingered on her finger; obviously from the cleaning product they used here. Two things. Three to go. The menu was well laid out and visually appealing. The décor was simple; dark tables and chairs, lightly coloured walls, a fridge with a glass door near the edge of the kitchen was filled with an array of different juices. There was nothing here that screamed kitsch faux-Japanese and somehow that was comforting.

"It all looks fine."

Beth waved to the waitress and ordered a simple salmon bento box.

"Karaage chicken with the seaweed salad. And I might have the Nasu Miso too." Reiko order the chicken because it was always reliable and it should be difficult to mess up a simple eggplant and miso dish. The waitress came back with some table water, and Beth leaned back in her chair.

"So tell me, Reiko, what happened between you and Yolande? Do I have a staff problem going forward?"

"What do you mean?" Reiko hadn't looked in the Seraph's group chat all day, and suddenly she dreaded what everyone might be saying about Yolande and her. Had she done her five things? Or only four? Her stomach sank, her body heavy with the weight of her mistakes.

"Yolande sent me a message."

"Oh?"

"She wanted to make sure you two were on different rosters."

Reiko frowned. "That isn't going to work." Reiko worked as kitty and behind the bar for every weekend night. What

Yolande was asking for meant that Yolande couldn't dance, didn't it?

"No. So tell me. What happened? And why were you sitting on the front steps looking so down?"

Reiko cleared her throat. "I fucked up. That's what happened."

"Are you sure? It doesn't seem like you." If only Beth knew the truth.

"Um, it's just like me." Or rather, it was exactly what Father would have done if he wanted something, and she'd done exactly the thing that always pissed her off when done to her.

"Reiko. What has happened? You are part of the team here, part of Seraph's family. Please let me help you?"

Reiko wanted to growl or laugh or run away. Yeah, definitely the last one. "You don't know me at all, so when you say it doesn't sound like me, you are wrong. I absolutely and definitely fucked things up with Yolande."

"I believe you. I'm just surprised. You always put everyone else first at work."

"I thought I was doing that this time too. She mentioned she was upset about her living situation and I gave her a solution."

Beth frowned. "I don't see the problem."

"She… quite rightly… suggested that I should have consulted with her first. She wanted to be involved in deciding the solution, not have me do it without asking her what she wanted." It was as vague as she could be without telling Beth that she'd bought a whole fucking apartment for them both.

Sitting here in a small sushi shop made her choice seem

even more problematic. She'd really overstepped, and she didn't know how to fix it. Could you even fix a hurt like that? Or would it always leave a scar? Even if Yolande accepted her apology, she'd always have the scar to remind her of this time.

"It sounds like you need to apologise and then communicate better with her. Try this: Hey Yolande, I'm really sorry for acting without asking you first. I'd really like to make amends. How can I do that?" Beth's suggestion sounded pretty good. Although…

"What if she doesn't accept my apology?"

"What if she does? She can't decide until you talk to her."

Reiko sighed, just as the waitress brought their food.

"Is there a problem?"

"Not with the food. Sorry." Her chicken smelled great, and the seaweed salad had the perfect texture. Even Beth's bento box looked really good; the salmon was smoked so freshness wasn't as much of an issue as if it'd been finely sliced fresh tuna or prawn or well, pretty much anything else. All around the food looked like a good choice; completely unlike her choice to buy Yolande a house. What the hell had she been thinking? It wasn't with her brain, that's for sure. Decisions made from the heart usually weren't rational. She broke apart the bamboo chopsticks and rubbed them together to get rid of splinters. Heart—whatever. It'd been all ego. She'd wanted to show off to her lover.

"I've been in love with Yolande for a long time." Admitting it out loud to Beth made all her muscles tense.

"I know."

"You do?"

"Reiko, I'm more than the boss at Seraph's. You are all my family. I watch you all carefully, and I've seen the way you look at her. I really thought she might have noticed, but then her mother died and she moved in with Helen. And I loved the way you respected her choice even when it obviously pained you every day."

Reiko stared at Beth. "You knew? Who else knew?"

"I don't think the others are as observant. They have their own concerns, but each of you is my concern."

"Did you know about Ace and Jack too?" Reiko had known Ace was in love with Jack—she had recognised the same yearning in him when he watched Jack dance—but had been surprised when Jack had reciprocated. There were some parallels there, not that Reiko wanted to spend any time thinking about it.

"Yes."

"Bloody dancers. Jack didn't notice Ace's love and Yolande didn't notice mine."

Beth chuckled. "They are used to being looked at with admiration. It's always going to take something special for them to notice when it's more personal." It made sense; Yolande had said as much at the wedding, that she'd been oblivious to Reiko and she regretted that.

"But that doesn't take away from the way I've messed up."

"No. You still need to apologise, and in a way that Yolande will understand. There is one other thing to consider as well."

"Oh?"

"For you, this love has been growing for a long time. For

Yolande, this is very new and fresh, so she will have a different perspective on it."

Reiko wanted to hide under the table. "Of course." A memory clanged in her head. Yolande had said as much, *"It was just one weekend. Not worth buying me a bloody house."*

"That doesn't mean it can't work out. Just that Yolande might need some time."

Reiko's face burned and she shoved the chicken in her mouth just to give herself something to do. Fried chicken; the perfect emotional food. There was nothing else to say. Beth was right. Reiko needed to apologise; not just for the house, but also for moving far too fast. She'd fallen hard since they'd kissed. Now she wanted to give Yolande everything. She wanted to use her money to make Yolande's life better, to give her all the choices that money could bring, and yet, she'd forgotten the core thing.

Choice couldn't be given. It had to be offered and Reiko had to take the risk that Yolande would say no. When she'd bought the house, she'd avoided the risk that Yolande would say no, because she'd assumed that Yolande would be so grateful that a yes was the only answer. By missing the point, Reiko had ended up with the no that she deserved. Somehow she got through the rest of lunch without having to talk much.

"I'll see you tomorrow for my shift." Reiko paid for them both, thanked the waitress for a lovely lunch, then walked outside.

"You'll apologise before then. I need Yolande on the bill." Beth's tone was all business, but her expression was soft as she pulled Reiko into a quick hug.

"Yes." Reiko waited as Beth crossed the road and walked

back inside Seraph's. She thumbed open her phone and sent a text.

Reiko: I'm really sorry for acting without asking for your opinion first.

She hit send before she could second guess it, then opened one of her rideshare apps to get a lift home. By the time the car arrived, her toes were jiggling in her shoes. Her hand slipped on the door handle as she opened it, and she had to wipe the clammy sweat off her palms before she could get into the car. As the car took her away from Seraph's and closer to home, she fought the urge to curl up in bed and ignore the world. Pretending to love from afar hadn't got her what she wanted. It had only been since the wedding that Yolande had noticed. A cynic would say that it was her money that made Yolande sit up and notice Reiko, but she shook off that thought quickly. If that was true, Yolande would have jumped at her house gift without any qualms.

Reiko: Thank you for being true to your principles, even when I couldn't be true to mine. I appreciate your honesty and I'm sorry that I overstepped in buying you a house without asking you first. The truth is…

Reiko paused, unsure if she was ready to write down the full truth. Her fingers twitched on the side of her phone and she accidentally sent the text. "Shit."

"Are you okay?" The driver asked.

"Yes." If okay meant accidentally sending a text before she'd finished it. She'd intended to delete the last sentence. It was too late now. She couldn't leave Yolande wondering about what the truth was. She tucked her phone into her pocket and closed her eyes. Perhaps if she ignored it, it wouldn't seem so odd.

Nearly a quarter of an hour later, the driver pulled up outside her building. "Here you are."

"Thank you." Reiko hopped out of the car, gave the driver five stars and a tip, then swiped into her building. Every step took time. Time that made her unfinished sentence weirder and weirder. She glanced at her phone and it confirmed everything. The unfinished sentence was worse because of the time that had passed.

Reiko: The truth is I've been in love with you for a long time.

She hit send before she could stop herself and let out a long trembling breath. Shit. It was done now. Time to have a shower and hide in her bed, away from the world. Regret would come soon enough.

17

Yolande grabbed her bag from her locker at the end of her shift and walked to her car. It was Murphy's fucking law that on the shift after a bad sleep, she'd have to work overtime. The early summer sunset hovered over the carpark. Nothing social media worthy, just another evening coming to an end while her body ached from standing on her feet all day in a surgery that went well over the scheduled time.

She slid into the driver's seat and just sat for a bit, too tired to drive just yet. Too tired to function. At least she wasn't due at Seraph's tonight. She sighed. Days like today were why she'd started dancing. She needed the release and joy that came with burlesque. She needed the energy of performance. Beth had been disappointed in her decision to have a break, and it nagged at her. Maybe she should go anyway. She really didn't like disappointing people. Slowly she realised that there was a difference between always saying yes to someone even when she didn't want to, and disappointing people when she said no. Why did she feel responsible for other people's feelings? Today's shitty day had overridden all the lingering emotions after she'd kicked Reiko out of her house. Why did it hurt so much?

She didn't want anyone to make decisions for her. Not anymore. But in the middle of the night, when it was dark and the minutes grew longer, she'd doubted everything. Their time together at the wedding had been so magical. And afterward the wedding, Reiko had called her every day after her shift to make sure she stayed awake driving home. Fuck, she needed that now. Tears pricked the corners of her eyes. Damn it. She'd already done enough crying over Reiko, so she pressed the heels of her hands against her eyes to push those bloody tears back inside. After a moment, she realised that she wanted to be home. To hug Bounce and hope that Captain would let her pat him. To rub her lucky crystal and wish for a better future.

Her crystal—saved from Helen by Reiko... Yeah, she didn't need the reminder of Reiko being so thrilled by their heist. Having it returned to her side was what mattered; the fact that getting it back had been so much fun and had resulted in the best sex of her life... Well, that wasn't something she was going to think about right now. The crystal had been in the bottom of her bag all day. Had having it nearby helped save their patient today? Hopefully. This type of bone deep weariness made it hard to function, except it was satisfying too because it came with a job well done.

She grabbed her bag and burrowed her hand into it to grab her crystal. Ah, there it was. Her fingers curled around it and the back of her hand brushed against her phone. She pulled out the crystal and held it against her breastbone for a moment, settling her pounding heartbeat. Eventually, she felt energised enough to pick up her phone.

Notifications filled the screen, so she opened it up to see messages from Beth and Steph asking about tonight, and a series of messages from Reiko. She read them slowly, her pulse speeding as the words sunk in deep.

Reiko understood what she'd done wrong, and the last one… Yolande swallowed. Reiko had loved her for years? Why hadn't she noticed? Her whole body stilled, wanting to move, to run to Reiko, but trapped by the overwhelming emotion that made her heart thud like the bassline in that Cardi B song. It'd been the first song Reiko had played at the beginning of their road trip. How could she feel so damned tired and so alive at the same time? With shaking fingers, she turned the key in the car and waited for the car to connect to her phone, then dialled Reiko.

"Hi." Reiko sounded breathy, like she'd run across the room to grab her phone.

"Um, I don't want to talk about it yet."

"Okay?"

"I know it's probably confusing, but I'm really tired and I was hoping you'd chat to me while I drove home."

"Okay. Are you ready to drive?" Reiko's voice softened.

"Yes. Just start talking about anything that isn't us."

Reiko cleared her throat. "Sure. I've been trying to write the synopsis for my PhD work. Do you want to hear about that?"

"I'd love to." Yolande needed a distraction, and she had no idea what Reiko was studying. It wasn't exactly a distraction because her heart sped up at the prospect of learning more about Reiko, and no, that probably wasn't something she wanted to think too hard about just now.

"Okay. So my thesis is a discussion on racism in the vegan movement…"

"It is? Is that a thing?"

"Definitely."

The passion in that one word was enough to keep Yolande alert. "Please tell me more." She began her drive home, keeping her gaze firmly on the road.

"Essentially there are two key reasons why the vegan movement is racist, and my thesis is focusing on the way the vegan movement attempts to homogenise culture by creating boundaries around the way people eat. Vegans create the notion that most cultures, particularly Indigenous cultures globally, are cruel because they eat an omnivorous diet, and of course, that's racism in action."

"Carry on."

"The way that different groups of people eat is related, largely, to the quality of soil where they live. Like, cultures that evolve on land which is highly fertile tend to eat more plant-based diets, while cultures from land that is lacking in fertility tend to eat more meat-based diets. It's easier to get food energy from meat when the soil lacks the ability to grow abundant fruit and vegetables. Most plants grown in low fertile soils are high in cellulose which humans can't process, while animals that are fully herbivorous can, meaning that getting food energy is a two stage process. The animal eats the high fibre plant and processes the cellulose, making their muscles filled with the nutrition from the plants. If a human then eats that animal, they gain access to the energy in the plant that they couldn't process themselves."

"I'm a nurse, Reiko. I understand basic nutrition." Yolande was too tired to hold back her irritation at having human biology explained to her.

"Fair enough. I'll skip to the important part." Reiko paused. "There is a privilege in vegans talking about only eating foods grown on highly fertile lands; for a start it's class- and wealth-based, so veganism is a diet that only the wealthy can afford. That results in the general type of racism based in the history of societal class around the world, which is a complex thing to explain. On a more obvious front, many vegan activists fight against the right of different cultures to eat a meat-based diet, even though that meat based diet has evolved with the culture due to the availability of a food source. The other important angle are the issues surrounding agriculture and who farms plants, because the majority of farm workers around the world who grow the food that vegans eat are people of colour. And the working conditions for many of those farm workers is at a low standard. Thus veganism is funded on the backs of disenfranchised workers."

"I had no idea it was so complex."

"All of life is complex."

Yolande grinned. "Very true. How did you get started on this topic?"

"My supervisor is interested in eating disorders, and she feels that any extreme diet, such as a vegan one, is an eating disorder. I won't go into the details of that since it's a tricky argument to make with many opinions around it. For my research, we started with idea that a vegan diet is one that only the privileged with plenty of money can afford, and we just extended that to look at the consequences. My research will highlight many examples from around the world of different groups of people, and how their traditional styles of food come into conflict with the ideals of veganism, and by extension how that leads to vegan activists making cruel and racist statements."

"That's pretty incredible research. I had no idea."

"Thanks. I'd rather not talk about the examples, because some of them are horrific and it's a big emotional load."

"No problems. What else did you do this week?"

"I had sushi with Beth at the place across the road from Seraph's." The drive passed quickly with Reiko's soothing voice pitched at just the right tone to keep her alert without adding any more tension to her already tense muscles. She parked her car on the street outside her apartment.

"Thank you."

"Same again tomorrow? Just text me with a time."

"Sure." Yolande waited until Reiko ended the call before letting out a big sigh. Were they just going to fall back into their old routine?

A week later, Yolande knew the answer.

Yes.

Yes, she wanted to have Reiko in her life. She wanted the routine they'd had before the wedding, with Reiko as her friend and personal 'keep alert' helper, and she wanted Reiko in her bed with the same joie de vivre they'd enjoyed at the wedding. Those few days away from the real world had been filled with so much emotion. In many ways, it hadn't felt real—a little magical, and surreal, and incredible. Was it even possible to feel that way again during day-to-day life? Yolande hoped so. More than that, she was ready to take the risk and find out.

Reiko had kept her company on her drive home from work every day, chatting about ordinary things in her soothing voice, and she'd continued to honour Yolande's wish to avoid talking about the house and Reiko's apology. But as time went on, Yolande realised that it was rude of her to make Reiko wait. She'd already accepted the apology days ago—in her mind anyway—so she needed to make it formal and let Reiko know the truth. She had the next two days off work, and she'd already resolved to meet with Beth and discuss getting back on Seraph's schedule. There was one thing she needed to do first.

Yolande: Thank you for apologising.

Reiko: I messed up. Of course I would apologise.

Yolande: I shouldn't have let you wait so long before telling you though.

Reiko sent a thumbs up emoji. Yolande's stomach grumbled a little, reminding her it was almost lunchtime.

Yolande: Want to catch up for lunch today?

Reiko: Now? Any preferences for where?

Yolande: I'll come to your place.

Reiko sent her address, even though Yolande already had it saved in her phone. She was still annoyed about the house —seriously who the fuck just went out and bought someone a house—but it didn't matter as much as the way Reiko made her feel cared for, like she mattered enough for her to ensure she drove home safely every day after work. Until

Reiko had started doing this, she hadn't realised how anxious she was about driving home, especially at night. It was logical that she would, since that was how her mum had died, but still. It was just… nice. No one else had ever done that for her. No one else had listened to her and known what she'd needed. Okay, so Reiko had also decided that a house was something she needed. Where should she draw the line?

If she was going to meet Reiko for lunch soon, she needed to get moving, so she grabbed her bag, patted the cats, then locked the house before walking to the tube. Driving to Reiko's place wasn't an option given London traffic and parking, while the tube was convenient and would take her close to Reiko's front door. An hour later, she regretted not grabbing a piece of fruit for the trip as her stomach ached with hunger, or probably just nerves? She pressed the buzzer for Reiko's flat.

"Come in." Reiko's voice was a little disembodied through the electronic system.

"Okay." Yolande could do this. She pushed open the glass doors and walked through the marbled atrium to the elevator and pushed the button for Reiko's floor. Imagine living here. It was like something in a luxury magazine. She checked and double checked her eye makeup and hair in the mirrored walls of the elevator as it flew up to the fifteenth floor. When the doors opened, she stepped out into a little hallway with three doors. One was for the fire escape stairs, while the other two had name plates. Yolande tapped her knuckles on Reiko's door just under the sign that said 'Inoue', and her toes tapped out the same rhythm in her shoe.

The door swung open.

"Welcome." Reiko stepped back and Yolande sucked in a short breath as she walked inside. "You can leave your bag there if you want." Was that a tremor in Reiko's voice?

"Thanks." Yolande dumped her bag on the small side table and automatically squirted some hand sanitiser on her palms and rubbed them together. The pandemic was over, yet she hadn't lost the habit. Would she ever? Reiko walked down the hallway and Yolande followed.

"Wow." She was unprepared for the incredible view that spread out before her. The lounge had floor to ceiling glass and a view over the Thames and Tower Bridge. "What an amazing view."

"Yes, I'm quite lucky."

Yolande gulped. She'd almost said that if she'd known what Reiko's place was like she would've just moved in. "It'd be pretty amazing at night too." She cringed a little. Now it sounded like she was trying to invite herself over at night. Her heartbeat thudded in her ears, too loud and with an urgency that she wanted to surrender to.

"It does. The building doesn't allow pets though, so it's not totally perfect."

"Speaking of which. Thank you for the house offer. I know I freaked out a bit…" Yolande swallowed again but Reiko didn't say anything. "Um, and it was quite a lot, but I've come to realise that you meant well."

Reiko shook her head. "Intentions don't matter if the result is hurt. I'm really sorry that I didn't ask you what you wanted. I shouldn't have acted without your consent."

"You do see the irony?"

Reiko rubbed her hands over her face. "Yes. Of course.

I've been beating myself up ever since you pointed out the obvious truth. I can't believe I did the exact thing that I've been mad at Father for doing to me my whole life."

"Don't beat yourself up. I'm so sorry that I made you feel less for trying to help me."

"No. I'm sorry that I hurt you while learning an important lesson. Please don't excuse me."

Yolande hated to see the way Reiko's face was drawn with tension and self-flagellation. She stepped forward and wrapped Reiko into a hug. As she held Reiko in her arms, she knew the truth. This was what she wanted. Her body relaxed, all the tensions of the last week easing out of her muscles, as Reiko leaned her head against Yolande's shoulder.

"It's going to be okay. Truly." Having Reiko in her arms cemented the way her heart settled into a strong steady beat. This was home. With Reiko. She wanted to come home to this hug after every shift, and only one thing would make it better. Bounce and Captain nudging her legs with their heads.

"Okay?"

"It really is going to be okay. More than okay." Yolande pressed a kiss to Reiko's forehead. Her lips against soft skin reminded her of their first kiss outside the little church in the Lake District and also held the promise of many more kisses in the future. "Because when people love each other, they forgive each other. They help each other grow and learn. I want to do that. I missed you, Reiko and I don't want to throw away what we have just because of this."

"You missed me?"

"Reiko. Are you fishing for compliments? You know you

don't need them." Yolande joked, then sighed. "I'm sorry. I often—"

"Make a joke when you are uncomfortable. I know. I often interrupt people when I'm emotionally overwhelmed."

"You do?"

Reiko swallowed. Was it bad that Yolande wanted to kiss her throat where it moved? No, but the timing wasn't the best.

"No. I used to do that and I'm trying to practice listening instead. I'm sorry that my listening turned into an action without consent."

"Enough of the sorry. What a sorry pair we are. I miss you, Reiko. I want to be with you. We've apologised enough, and now I just want a kiss." She'd made the decision to be forthright in outlining what she wanted.

"I want a kiss too." Reiko tipped her head up with her lips slightly parted. The tiniest glimpse of her pink tongue sent a flush across Yolande's face. There was only one thing to do. She kissed Reiko and poured all her hopes into the kiss. Reiko clung to her, her fingers digging into her scalp, tight enough to be almost painful, and still her mouth opened and together they deepened the kiss. It was as though they couldn't get close enough to each other, both needing to be inside each other, with a desperation that reminded Yolande of the best nights in the Peacock room.

"My bedroom is to your left." Reiko nudged her leg between Yolande's to guide her and she used her dance skills, letting Reiko lead her. Clothes flew off as they walked and by the time, Yolande broke their kiss to remove her shirt—a necessity—she was lost to sensation. It didn't matter where she was, provided she would get to kiss Reiko everywhere.

She spread her hands all over Reiko, her familiar body and scent filling her senses. Touch, taste, and the irregular pants of Reiko's breath as she responded to every stroke of Yolande's fingers. Yolande explored. She wanted to carve Reiko's shape into her memory; not just the way she was now as a nearly-thirty-year-old woman, but her very bone structure so she would always know her even when they were both old. Yolande gasped.

"What is the matter?"

"I think I love you." Yolande had had an inkling that this might come eventually. Not yet. It was too soon.

"Oh?"

"I know you said it already in a text and I haven't acknowledged that. It's been too soon."

Reiko nodded. "Beth said as much. She said I should be patient because we were on different journeys."

"What does that mean?" Yolande lifted her head, for the first time, seeing Reiko's bedroom. The staggering view with all those glass windows continued. Imagine waking up here.

"It means I've been in love with you for a long time, Yolande, and for you, this is new."

"It is new." Yolande cupped Reiko's cheek and gently stroked her thumb over the edge of her eye where she'd twitched inadvertently. "I didn't want to be in another relationship so soon. I wanted to spend time getting to know what I wanted, and yet, this is exactly what I want. Love doesn't have a perfect time, or the right pace, or whatever. I want to be with you. Here." She glanced out of the window and gulped. "Or wherever it is that is with you."

"I'd like that very much." Reiko gave her a little push and they tumbled together onto the bed. Reiko straddled her as she kissed her. Soon it was all tongue and lips and kisses and hands everywhere as they rolled and tumbled together on Reiko's luxurious huge bed. When Reiko pushed her hands inside Yolande's pants, she cursed breathlessly.

Yolande grabbed the waistband of her own pants and shoved them down over her hips, then reached for Reiko's clothes to help her pull them off too. Now that Yolande had declared herself, there was no need for patience anymore. No reason for delicacy. She wanted to devour Reiko, and it seemed Reiko wanted to do the same. Soon enough, Reiko had two fingers inside her, and Yolande could already feel the delicious pressure building. Sex with someone she loved was better, more intense because of the emotional connection, and nothing that came before this moment mattered anymore. This was her future. Her now and her forever.

She pulled Reiko's face closer and kissed her again, bucking as Reiko pressed the heel of her hand against her clit. Holy. Electricity flooded her veins and her skin felt alight. The musky scent of arousal filled the air, and she sank her teeth into Reiko's shoulder as Reiko pumped with one hand and teased her clit with the other.

"Oh yes. Now. Now." Yolande cried out, choking as pleasure overtook her. Waves of sensation surrounded her as she shattered under Reiko's ministrations.

She was still trembling when Reiko lifted her hand to her mouth and dragged her wet fingers across her lips. The salty taste of her orgasm shook her again, and she sucked Reiko's fingers into her mouth. Reiko moaned and Yolande grabbed her bare bottom, sinking her fingers between Reiko's legs until she found the wetness she sought. Her fingers were shaking so hard with her own orgasm that she could barely do anything more than just fumble around for Reiko's clit. Luckily Reiko didn't need much, not judging by the way she groaned and moaned and pushed her body against Yolande's hand.

"I fucking love you Reiko." Each word was hoarse. It didn't matter.

Reiko pulled Yolande close as she clamped around her fingers. They lay there, collapsed on the bed, with the sun streaming in the giant windows until Yolande's stomach grumbled.

EPILOGUE

Yolande guided Reiko into their apartment. Yes, they'd bought an apartment that they both loved, and now Reiko stood in the lounge wearing a silk scarf as a blindfold. It was sensual and gave Yolande far too many ideas, but first she had a surprise for Reiko. They'd gone away for a week's holiday in Scotland while the contractors had finished creating this final masterpiece for their apartment.

"Can I look yet?" Reiko leaned against Yolande. Yolande swallowed the lump in her throat.

"Soon, my love, soon." She shouldn't be nervous about this, they'd already joked about it on their trip, and she was pretty sure Reiko would've already bought her a ring if she didn't still feel guilty about the whole house fiasco. Today, Yolande would make her choice clear.

"I don't see why you need to do this," Reiko said.

"The cat run that Elle designed is complete and I want you to be the first person who sees Captain and Bounce explore it." Yolande had been thrilled when the interior designer Reiko had employed, Elle Denbigh-Yadav, had suggested a cat run for the whole apartment, with a fully enclosed section on the balcony so the cats could go outside without disturbing the bird life. It was an excuse, a poor one, to get Reiko in a blindfold.

"Okay."

"Wait there for a second." Yolande moved away from Reiko and opened the cage with Captain in it. He strutted out and Yolande picked him up. She quickly tied the ribbon holding the ring box around his neck, and he squirmed in her arms, unhappy about the idea. Typical grumpy cat.

"Hold out your hands." Yolande placed Captain in Reiko's arms, then removed the blindfold. Reiko blinked a few times, then stared around the room.

"Oh, it looks incredible. Even better in real life than the plans." Reiko grinned, then glanced down at Captain, ready to place him on one of the sections of the cat run. She stroked her hand over his head, frowning slightly as her fingers touched the ribbon Yolande had tied around his neck. The ribbon was connected to a little ring box that held…

"Go on, open it."

"What is this?" Reiko untied the ribbon and held the attached box awkwardly. Captain was a big cat and it took both of Reiko's arms to hold him. Yolande grimaced; she should have realised this before she came up with this plan.

"Shall I take Captain?"

"No. Take the box. What is it?"

"I know we've only been living together for six months, but it's been the best six months of my life and…" Yolande knelt down in front of Reiko and opened the box, showing her the ring with a blue agate crystal. "Please marry me. You are the love of my life and I want to spend the rest of my days with you."

Reiko's cheeks blushed bright pink and a slow smile spread across her face. "Yes, please."

"So polite."

"Should I be ruder?" Reiko's voice cracked a little. She bent down and let Captain leap out of her arms, before standing straight again.

"Only if you want me to ravage you with that blindfold."

"Oh, yes please. Today and every day." Her quiet Reiko hadn't changed but she had shown a rather inventive bold side in bed, and Yolande adored that Reiko reserved that just for her. Yolande stood up and kissed Reiko.

Yolande was home now. She'd found love with someone who respected her opinions and cared for her and never dismissed her needs. She'd only ever had her mum as a family, which hadn't been a lack. Now she had Reiko, and all the Seraph's crew, and she poured all her joy into this kiss.

"You know what this means though?" Reiko shook her head.

"What?"

"My parents are going to want to throw the wedding of the century."

"Shall we foil them and get married at the registry tomorrow?"

Reiko laughed. "As tempting as that is, the crew at Seraph's missed out on Helen's extravagant wedding. Let's give them all a weekend to remember."

And that was why Yolande loved Reiko. "Look at you.

Always thinking about how to make life special for other people."

"It's not completely unselfish. I will get to marry the love of my life." Reiko winked and it was the most natural thing in the world to kiss her again. And again. Forever.

~

If you enjoyed this book, you'll love the next book in the Seraph's Burlesque Club series, SHOW OFF.

Burlesque dancer Charlie Kent should be happy performing and hooking up with sexy people now the pandemic is over. Instead it feels empty as the audience is always missing Elle, her friend-with-benefits. They were just casual, but Charlie now realises she wants more. Much more. When Elle arrives at the Seraph's Burlesque Club for business only, Charlie is not going to let this second chance go to waste.

Elle has sworn she's not going back to how things were before. Her interior design business certainly hasn't, with so much work she's barely thought of the sexy-as-sin burlesque dancer who she used to hook up with... Except when she's lonely all night. But she can't be just friends anymore, so she stays away. When she is commissioned to refit Seraph's Burlesque Club, Elle bumps into Charlie, and all her best intentions go out of the perfectly dressed window.

Elle must keep her professional reputation intact, and can't allow her attraction to Charlie to derail her work and her need for love. . . Unless she can have it all?

Want a bit more sexy romance and to see what happens at Reiko and Yolande's wedding? The wedding is available as an exclusive bonus when you sign up for my newsletter.

ACKNOWLEDGMENTS

I pay my respects to the Wangal people of the Eora Nation, who are the traditional owners of the land on which this book was written.

Thank you to Porcelain Alice and the team at Sky Sirens for all your help in my burlesque research. I'm sorry about the chair. I'm also incredibly grateful to burlesque dancer and sex worker TdC, who wished to remain anonymous in the acknowledgements, for all your research assistance around the junction between burlesque, stripping, and other sex work. I love TdC's quote, "Burlesque is all about finding your inner feminine power and using that to your advantage."

MV Ellis, Lina, and the rest of my writing buddies, Charity and Dianne, the Lesbian Campfire group and the Word Count Warriors at RWAus.

Thank you to Ali, Torrance, Marie, and Kait who have been wonderful emotional support while writing and editing this series.

Thank you to my friends Reiko and Yolande who

allowed me to use their names in this book. We were having coffee one morning and I complained that I'd run out of good names to use for characters. They told me that I could use their names, provided the characters were nothing like them.

AUTHOR NOTES

While this book is set in London, I wrote it from Australia. Writing a post-pandemic world where everyone is vaccinated is a type of contemporary fantasy, especially given the timing of when I wrote it (early 2021). For the most part, I've tried to keep the pandemic out of the story, and only allude to the impacts on the characters.

The global vaccination effort began in late December 2020, and at the time of writing, the pandemic was still having a major impact on life in USA, UK, Europe and other parts of the world. In Australia, we missed the worst of COVID, even with the Delta outbreak in June 2021. Having no land borders with any other country, comparatively good border quarantine systems, and being far from the rest of the world were all factors. Most Australians were willing to take steps to prevent the spread of COVID to protect our health care system, and this also worked well. The downside of this is that our government was slow with the vaccine rollout and even though I booked to get vaccinated as soon as I could, I wasn't fully vaccinated until September 2021.

As at October 2021, 1,653 Australians had died from COVID during the pandemic (and nearly five million people globally). One of the hardest things for many of my friends, acquaintances, and colleagues was the distance and lack of ability to travel. A large portion of my friends are immigrants to Australia. Several of them had close relatives die of COVID and were unable to travel to visit family or go to funerals.

I've made the deliberate choice to keep the pandemic in the background of the book. The impact of the pandemic on readers of this book is likely to be difficult and I write to give people hope, so I've tried to keep the worst of it off the page.

ALL BOOKS BY RENÉE DAHLIA

Thanks for reading SHOW UP. I hope you enjoyed it. Reviews can help readers find books, and I am grateful for all honest reviews. Thank you for taking the time to let others know what you've read, and what you thought. If you write a review for SHOW UP and email me with the link, I will send you a free copy of the second book in the series, SHOW OFF. My email is renee at reneedahlia dot com.

If you'd like to know more about me, my books, or to connect with me online, you can visit my webpage www. reneedahlia.com and if you sign up to my newsletter, you can grab a free book.

Twitter https://twitter.com/dekabat

Facebook https://www.facebook.com/reneedahliawriter/

Instagram https://www. instagram.com/reneedahlia_author/

You've just read a book in my Seraph's Burlesque Club Series.

Contemporary Series: Seraph's Burlesque Club

1. Show Up (ff with bisexual heroine)
2. Show Off (ff with bisexual heroine)
3. Show Queen (ff)
4. TBA Duo of Novellas (mm)

Contemporary Series: Kapow!

1. Out of Her League (fm with bisexual characters)
2. His Buxom Beauty (fm)
3. Craving His Spotlight (mm)
4. Her Pregnant Rival (ff)

Contemporary Series: Farrellton Foster Family

1. Betrayed (fm)
2. Forbidden (fm with bisexual characters)
3. Liability (ff)

Contemporary Series: Margaret River TV: Boxed Set

- Homage (fm with bisexual heroine)
- Uplift (ff with bisexual heroines)

Contemporary Series: Merindah Park

1. Merindah Park (fm)
2. Making Her Mark (fm with bisexual heroine)
3. Two Hearts Healing (fm)
4. Racetrack Royalty (fm)

Contemporary Series: Rainbow Cove

1. His Christmas Pearl (fm)
2. His Christmas Pride (mm)

Historical Series: Great War

1. Her Lady's Melody (ff)
2. Her Lady's Fortune (ff)
3. Her Lady's Honor (ff)
4. His Lord's Soldier (mm)

Historical Series: Bluestockings

Prequel: The Shipwrecked Earl's Bride (fm with bisexual hero)

1. To Charm a Bluestocking (fm with bisexual hero)
2. In Pursuit of a Bluestocking (fm)
3. The Heart of a Bluestocking (fm)